Unforgettable

No Ordinary Family Book 1

LINDA BARRETT

JC

DEDICATION

To my sister,

The one person who shares my childhood memories.

Love you, Judy!

AUTHOR'S NOTE

I started writing the *No Ordinary Family* series before Covid-19 upended our lives. In this first story, the Big Apple is thriving and Broadway is attracting crowds. Let's hope for a time very soon when every theater and concert venue across our country will be filled with cheering audiences once more.

Cover art by Shelley Kay at Web Crafters

E-book and print formatting by Web Crafters

www.webcraftersdesign.com

CHAPTER ONE

April—New York

Doug Collins paced the floor of his small apartment in New York City, his eyes drawn repeatedly to the pile of papers on his desk. Two hundred sheets, stacked neat and square, title page on top.

Stepping closer, he loomed over his work. Not the usual fare for a playwright, this novel--but it was finally complete. Finished. His fist came down hard on the manuscript. Finished? Then where was the satisfaction he longed for? Where was the closure? He stroked the top page in atonement and smiled ruefully. Closure? Not with that title:

STRAIGHT FROM THE HEART...
...a love story in search of an ending...

He and Jen. How could the story's inspiration be anyone else?

Jennifer Grace Delaney. She was either his inspiration or his albatross. While students together at Boston University, she'd been the quiet girl in the back of the English class who'd captured his heart with her first essay--writing filled with pain, strength, and wrapped in love. Goosebumps had covered his skin as he'd read her words aloud to the class in a random exchange of student essays. They covered him now, as he recalled their honesty. But she'd hated that class. Said personal stories belonged in a private diary, not exposed to a bunch of strangers. She'd stick to numbers.

She'd loved him, too. Believed in him. They'd planned a future...at least he'd thought they had...but in the end, she wouldn't leave her siblings.

His breath jerked at the memory. They could have had the perfect life: Wall Street for Jen; Broadway for him. Or rather off-off Broadway back then. Serious theater. He'd lined up a bartending job at night, too. He'd thought Jen was onboard.

But on the day after graduation, she'd met him in Boston Common with shadowed eyes and a forced smile.

"What's wrong, Henny-Penny?"

Avoiding his gaze, she'd said, "I'm not good at beating around the bush, so I'll just come out with it." She'd finally looked at him. "I've taken the position with Fidelity here in Boston. I can't leave my family. I can't move to New York."

He stared, frozen. "How could you make such an important decision without discussing it first—with me? We're the two that count here."

"I know," she said softly, "but I couldn't take the chance that you'd change my mind. I'm so torn inside. I want to go, but I just can't leave Lisa to manage everything. The boys are a teenage handful and Emily...well, you know sweet Em. Still not the most confident kid on the block."

Her generous heart. He loved her for it, but... "Sometimes, Jen, loyalty can go too far. Your big sister's not alone. There are two adults in that house."

Her mouth wobbled, and she reached for his hand. "Technically, yes. But Mike and Lisa...? I don't know. Something's not right between them. I can feel it. I'm uneasy. They leave notes for each other and don't talk. Mike comes home late often, and I think he's out with his team, hitting some clubs. He never used to do that. He and Lisa..."

She paused, and he saw her gasp for breath.

"...seem to be living two separate lives in one house. I don't know what's happened or what's going to happen, and I-I just can't leave my brothers and sisters now. They're too young. They need me."

Silence pulsed against his ears. "Have you spoken with Lisa directly?"

"I can't," she whispered. "Lisa's so private. She thinks she's protecting us. And really, their marriage isn't my business. Mike's been very good to me. To all of us." She shrugged. "It's just...he's gone so often during the season, and now he's gone at night in the off-season. All I know is that Lisa's got too much on her plate."

"All marriages have tough times. They'll work it out."

"Maybe so," she admitted, "but I know what I see and feel. Threads are fraying--again. She rose from their bench and gazed into the distance. "The timing is wrong for us. But maybe we can find some weekends to visit. It's a short flight, right?" She faced him again, her eyes welling. "Maybe when the kids are older, I'd feel better about leaving them. Please, Doug, please don't argue with me."

Damn! Was she just going to fold like that? She was twenty-two now, a college graduate. An adult.

"What about us, Jen? An occasional weekend is not a real life! You're entitled to your freedom."

Her chin had come up, the threat of tears gone, her violet eyes now almost sizzling black. "Am I really? After everything she's given up for us--me and the little ones? I-I can't leave her to cope alone. I'm the next oldest. I love them, and I...owe them!"

His blood ran hot, but his stomach knotted in cold fear. If he was going to lose this argument, he wouldn't go down easy.

"Can't leave them or won't? Tell me, Jen, for how many years does the accident reverberate? For how many years is it allowed to control you? You're the math genius, so what's the answer?"

She froze for a moment, then cupped his cheek. "You already know the answer," she whispered. "Deep inside...that place where truth lives."

He flinched now as he recalled her words. His words. He'd used them on her after reading that essay, the one that had blown him away.

Now the tears ran down her cheek as she spoke. "I'm so sorry, Doug. I'm sorry for us both. But my family has to come first. The Delaney siblings either stick together or fall. That's what I've learned. If we'd been separated back then, after the accident...well, we wouldn't have survived, not as a family." She kissed him quickly. "It won't be forever. Maybe one day, you'll be able to write again in Boston. We'll talk on the phone. We'll visit on weekends."

He knew she was grasping for a thread of salvation, but he was, too. "I love you, Jen. Don't disappear on me."

Then she'd kissed him and run off, leaving him to stare in disbelief.

He rubbed his damp forehead as the image of a racing Jennifer, long hair flying, remained in his mind's eye. The emotions remained, too. Love, disappointment, anger, frustration—he'd wanted to smash something. Writing a scene, he'd discovered, was a hell of a lot easier than living through one.

Patting the manuscript on his desk, he collapsed into the chair in front of the computer.

He'd called Jen every Sunday in the beginning. She flew down once, met a couple of his friends--other writers. He'd hoped to change her mind, convince her to take a chance in the Big Apple. "You could have stayed in Boston," she'd countered. But that wasn't true. Not with his hard-won residency with Playwrights' House— an opportunity of a lifetime.

The visits became fewer, the phone calls less frequent. Busy careers. Busier lives. Both trying to make their marks.

But dammit! Five years in limbo was long enough!

He tapped the keyboard and composed an email to his friend, editor Steven Kantor. The man was doing him a favor by reading a manuscript not for publication. Steve wouldn't earn a dime, even if he loved it. But maybe that's what goosed the editor's curiosity. He knew Doug's plays—his emergence as a serious playwright—heck, the guys had been friends for five years, hitting New York at about the same time, both craving success and working non-stop.

"If you wrote it," Steve had said, "it won't be a time-waster. Just send it when you're ready. Maybe I'll learn something."

A compliment like that couldn't be bought. Doug gifted him with tickets to any Broadway show he wanted.

He skimmed the manuscript pages one more time. Then, attaching the electronic file to his email, he took a deep breath and hit Send.

It was time to let Jen go. Or find her again.

##

One month later—Boston

On a late Friday afternoon in May, Jennifer Delaney hung up the phone—hopefully the last call of the day—and walked to her office window, amazed, as always, at how lucky she'd been. A wonderful career, great friends…not to mention the stunning view of Boston Harbor.

The huge investment firm where she worked suited her to a T. Helping to manage funds and advising clients about risk soothed their money worries as well as her own. Sighing, she acknowledged how ridiculous that seemed now. Her checkbook, her personal investments were sound. She wondered why childhood scars were so hard to heal.

Losing loving parents at sixteen…unspeakable pain. But she'd survived. Her older sister and brother-in-law thought she'd thrived. Her younger siblings thought she was cool. Maybe she was! Regardless, they'd had each other's backs from the beginning of those rough days and always would. She couldn't imagine her life without them. Her life was good. Calm. Balanced. Like her checkbook. "Just the way I want it to be," she murmured.

Her phone rang again. Shaking her head, she raced back to her desk. "Jennifer Delaney speaking."

"How are you, Henny-Penny?"

That voice. The receiver slipped from her hand and hit the floor. That warm voice. That nickname. Once upon a time...

Retrieving the phone, she said, "I'm well. Doing very well, thanks. It's been a long time...so, how's New York?"

"New York was humming along the last I saw it. And that's the thing, Jen. I'm back in Boston now, and I'd love to see you. Any chance you're free tonight? The workday's almost over."

Back in Boston? Like forever or just a quick visit? Their parting might have been her decision years ago, but the pain afterward? She couldn't go through that kind of heartache again, she decided. Better to bail quickly.

"Sorry, I've already got plans for tonight. But I hope you enjoy your visit."

She disconnected and took a deep breath. She'd been polite, her voice steady. Good job. When the phone rang again, she glanced at the readout, took another—deeper—breath before answering. "Let's blame a poor connection. I've got plans for tonight," she repeated.

"How about tomorrow? Saturday."

She gripped the receiver as though it were a life preserver. "Afraid not. I'm booked."

"Is that right?"

"In fact, I'm looking at my calendar right now," she said, with a quick glance at it, "and every day has something scheduled. I'm sorry, but I've really gotta go. As I said before, have a nice visit."

Replacing the phone gently in the cradle, she shivered. A whole body shiver. She hadn't lied. Her life was busy—and calm—just the way she liked it. She and Doug had simply drifted apart, following their own paths in their own worlds. At this point, she didn't need any emotional upheavals. She studied her computer screen, and in minutes, she was once again Jennifer Delaney, happy career woman.

##

At five-thirty, Jen was surrounded by co-workers who'd become friends, all set to kick back and hit the clubs. That's what twentysomethings did on a Friday night in Boston. And she loved a good time as much as anyone.

"I'm just about ready," she said, smiling, as she logged out of her computer. They stood outside her office door—two guys and two gals—all trying to prove themselves, but still believing the theory about all work and no play. Her friends were certainly not dull. Not these bright, energetic, career-minded people. They were her friends for a reason!

She changed her high heels for flat sandals, grabbed her purse, rose and joined the others. "I'm hungry. Where are we eating?"

Alexis laughed, her brown eyes shining. "You mean we're not sampling the freebies at every bar's happy hour and saving on dinner?"

"Oh, geez. I'm not that bad, am I?" Jen protested.

Her friends simply stared. "When it comes to spending money, let's just say—you're frugal," said Alexis.

She held up her hands. "Okay, okay…guilty as charged."

"Not that we're complaining," chimed in Liz, with a chuckle. "Living in Beantown is expensive, and saving is a challenge."

"Well, I'm conceding right now," said Matthew. "Some of us need real food! Not just peanuts."

"Then go home to your mama, and get a good meal," said Liz, reaching up to pat him on the shoulder.

Everyone laughed as they piled into the elevator, but Jen sensed new vibes. Matt and Liz. The young woman's gentle teasing, her tender touching was becoming a habit.

The elevator deposited them in the spacious marble lobby of the building, and the group headed toward the plate glass doors leading to the plaza outside.

"The days are getting longer and warmer," said Matt, holding the door open for the others, "which means our playtime is longer, too."

The chatter continued, but when Jen stepped outside, she heard nothing more, and saw nothing except the tall man with a hank of dark hair falling over his forehead, the man whom she'd once labeled skinny but wasn't anymore, the man who'd once held her heart. Surprise held her frozen until a slow anger warmed her up.

She watched him, and by his stillness, identified the moment he spotted her. One second, two seconds. He waited, but made no move toward her, as though afraid she'd disappear.

Then came the smile, the smile that once had melted her heart. She used to run her fingers over his mouth, outlining his lips, kissing them. But that was then...

Her hands clenched into fists as he finally approached. She moved closer to her friends.

"Hang on a sec," she whispered, her throat dry.

They halted instantly.

"What's wrong, Jen?"

She couldn't speak. Doug was only six feet from them now, filling her vision. And suddenly, he was there. Right in front of her.

"Hello, Jennifer Grace Delaney. I've missed you."

No! Taller, bigger than in her memory. And his eyes, still so dark, darker than a moonless night is how she used to think of them. A kaleidoscope of remembrances hit her at once, and her initial anger ebbed, replaced by an eon of past loneliness and disappointment. And right now, fear. She wouldn't survive a repetition of the past.

"Who is this guy?" Her four friends surrounded her.

She gulped some air, raised her chin. "Someone I used to know. An old college…uh…classmate."

##

Her friends were astute. Their eyes focused on him, then Jen, their curiosity apparent. He didn't care about her friends—what they saw, heard or thought. Only Jen was real. And more beautiful than in his dreams.

"An old classmate, huh?" he repeated. "That's a funny way to describe what we had." He focused on her face. "This guy," he said, echoing her friend's question, "is the man who can't forget you."

Her eyelids slammed shut, her mouth trembled before tightening. When she opened her eyes again, however, her gaze was steady. "It's been years, Doug. As the saying goes, 'that was then, this is now.' Maybe you need to try harder to…ah…forget."

"I've moved back, Jen."

"No, no, you haven't," she countered, her surprise laced with confusion. Returning didn't make sense at all. "Playwrights live in New York. We tried once, and it didn't work. I'm sorry, Doug, but I've moved on. She turned toward her friends. "It's time to leave. We're all starving."

Not yet. Not without him. He held out both hands, palms up. "Eight million people in New York," he said, slightly bouncing his left hand. "And one Henny-Penny here." He lifted his right arm high. "No contest."

She shrugged. "You didn't think so back then. You're very good with words, images and make-believe. While I, in case you've forgotten, deal with real people."

"I know."

She stepped toward him, her purse falling to the ground, her friends closing ranks behind her. "Real people, Collins, like the Delaney family. Not your ordinary kind of family. Just a bunch of kids trying to survive."

Good. Talk to me. Keep on talking. Communication is everything.

Before he could say a word, she turned to her friends again. A girl handed her the purse. "Sorry for the drama," Jen said. "It's the way he makes his living. He's good at it."

"Him? What about you?" a guy said. "A new side of the mysterious Jennifer Delaney."

So, he'd gotten to her, past her defenses. He wanted to cheer. The men were merely co-workers. If they thought of her as mysterious, she'd kept her private life private. Which meant no boyfriends. Regardless of what she'd said earlier, she hadn't moved on.

Which gave him hope.

Now all he needed was a little *chutzpah* to make his next move and be accepted by Jen's friends. "I remember a great club near here," he said, deliberately placing himself in the middle of the group. "Lots of eats, lots of music, and a karaoke bar."

Jen had turned away, but he saw her stiffen. Tapping her on the shoulder, he said, "You know we'll have fun. At least a song or two. Come on, Jen...I dare you."

##

Dare her? Like in the old days, except those were happy times with music and a microphone. Right now, she wanted the privacy of her own apartment. She needed to regain her equilibrium, to brace herself for whatever came next. But if she left, Doug would accuse her of running away. Again.

Pasting a smile on her face, Jen said, "All that goofing around in college? Nah. I don't do that anymore."

She threw a speaking glance at her girlfriends. They loved to kick back at the sing-along karaoke bars. Jen had the real voice, but they all had fun. Now, however, she knew her pals would cover for her.

"Then prove it," said Doug.

"What?"

He was shaking his head. "You always enjoyed being on a cozy stage. I can't believe you've changed that much. And you're good! Let's go to a club, Jen. For old times' sake. After all, I am new in town...."

"Oh, pu-leeze," she shot back. "You know this city like a native."

"It's been a few years."

She turned to the others. "I'm sorry about all this. Do you mind if we skip the pubs and go right to Maguire's? Real food for the starving plus live music, and then I'll go home. I've got an early choir rehearsal tomorrow anyway."

"I don't like this situation," said Evan, a quiet type who missed nothing. "Just say the word, Jen, and we'll get rid of..."

Oh, no! She patted the man's arm. "I'm fine, Evan. Really. He's not dangerous, except with a pen!" She smiled at him. "But thanks."

Five years building a life, and in five minutes, Doug Collins could tear it down. She couldn't chance another disappointment. Why had he come back after all this time? Glancing at her watch, she sighed. One hour or so was all she'd have to endure.

##

The Irish bar was filling up, but they managed to get a booth for six immediately. Jen sighed again, happy with their good luck, happy to keep to her one-hour plan.

Almost as immediately, Doug seemed comfortable with the group and made her friends feel comfortable with him. Not surprising. He had always been the proverbial "people person." She'd credit his many psychology courses.

Evan's quiet voice, however, managed to interrupt the general conversation about the menu and music. "So, Collins, what brings you back to Boston?"

A curious silence descended, and for the first time, Doug seemed to search for words. Jen's ears perked up.

"Let's say," he began slowly, "a couple of new projects and one item of unfinished business. Very important unfinished business." From diagonally across the table, he shifted toward Jen, his eyes capturing hers.

She sat straighter. "If you mean me, you're mistaken," she said, leaning forward, arms on the table. "Our 'business,' as you call it, is over. Nothing personal—though I guess you'd think it was—but I'm not looking for a relationship with you or anyone else. Just not my thing." *Not anymore.*

The quality of the following silence morphed from curious to deafening. She realized that in all her years with the company, she'd revealed more about herself just then than ever before. And now to prevent speculation—and gossip—she'd have to explain.

She glanced around the table, finding sympathy laced with curiosity in her friends' expressions. Okay.

She could handle that. Her message, however, was meant for Doug. She returned her gaze to him.

"In my world," she began, "people leave. First my parents—and you have no idea what that was like—and then you, and I wasn't sure about Mike and Lisa staying together either. I know you have to accept what's out of your control, like a car accident on an icy road. But I'm not going to volunteer for more heartache and grief. My life is great as it is. Your being in Boston is totally immaterial to me."

"Then it seems," he said softly, "that I have a lot of work to do."

The waitress approached, and conversation turned to food and drink. "Just a cup of chicken soup," said Jen. "I've lost my appetite."

"Maybe him tagging along wasn't a good idea," said Evan, nodding toward Doug. "You've managed to upset Jen, who's a very cool woman. So, let's get the whole picture. Why else are you here? What kind of projects?"

Jen looked at her co-worker. Who would have thought that this quiet guy would speak up now? Still waters....?

Doug shifted in his seat. His gaze swept both sides of the booth. "I'm a writer. I worked hard and got lucky, too. I have a new play, and its debut will be here with the Commonwealth Regional Theater company. And that's as far as I'm thinking."

Jen heard nothing after Commonwealth. Her choir, The All-City Chorus, rehearsed at that theater twice a week, and she'd be there in the morning. "'Of all the gin joints...'" she murmured.

She'd never doubted his talent, and she'd been right. His very first play had been staged in college. A rare honor. He'd been thrilled, of course, but shy about it. He used to say that writers were too insecure to brag.

And now, he'd been modest in front of her friends. It seemed he'd been totally focused on his craft while living in New York.

"Congratulations," she offered. "Sounds like you'll be busy with rehearsals and whatever—for a little while, and after a successful run here, poof! Back to Broadway. Works well for me."

"Writing your own script, Jen?" Doug's eyes gleamed. "Sorry to disappoint. I didn't renew the lease on my New York apartment because….I'm also this year's playwright-in-residence at our alma mater. If *The Sanctuary* goes to Broadway, I'll commute."

She needed air.

"I'm back, Jen. And tomorrow I'm hunting for new digs. I can't stay with my sister indefinitely. Any suggestions?" His glance traveled from Jen to the others, and she sighed in relief at the change of topic. An objective, neutral topic. Boston sported a dozen or more neighborhoods attractive to singles.

"It really depends on your budget," said Liz. "In this town, a one-bedroom can run anywhere from sixteen hundred to double that a month."

"I'd like to be close to the theater, if possible."

"Then that would be downtown," said Evan slowly. "A great choice."

Could the night get any worse? First the theater, now Jen's neighborhood—a walking neighborhood where she could run into him at any time. "I doubt he can afford it."

In unison, all eyes turned toward first toward her, then toward Doug.

"She's got a point, man," said Even. "But there are other great locations."

"There sure are," said Jen calmly now. "Many good areas. You don't need to be downtown."

Doug's eyes narrowed. "Any particular reason, Henny-Penny?"

Liz coughed and hid her mouth. Matt looked away. Not a shred of acting material in them.

"No reason at all." Jen waved her arm in dismissal. "Search the whole city. Means nothing to me if you go into debt." Deflection might work.

"For crying out loud, I might have known," said Doug with a sigh. "The starving playwright thing…. Well, I'm not quite there, and you don't have to worry I'll be asking for a loan. I do know how to budget." He chuckled and looked around the table, making eye contact with each person for a moment. "Although I seem to be in a minority among the financial whizzes here."

Everyone laughed. "Financial whizzes believe in budgets, too," said Liz.

"Who knows?" Doug said. "One day soon, I might be asking for advice."

And that's when Jen knew that Doug had turned her friends into his friends, too.

CHAPTER TWO

Jen signed her bill and got ready to leave. Hanging around for an evening with Doug was not going to happen. And she *did* have a rehearsal in the morning—not that an early start time had ever impeded her evening activities in the past.

"Hang on a sec. Look, Jen, karaoke's about to start. Go on. Sing. Remember way back one Christmas in Woodhaven…?"

Oh, God. Don't go there…don't go back to a time when happy endings beckoned. When she used to look as eager and hopeful as Doug did right now!

Would it be easier to sing something and put an end to all this nonsense? As a kaleidoscope of titles flashed through her mind, she smiled her herself. Perfect. She'd send him a musical message.

"If you're sure you want a song from me, okay. But don't complain afterwards." Escaping the booth, she quickly made her way to the emcee. He worked the gig every weekend and knew her.

"Jennifer Delaney! Lucky us," he greeted her, handing her the mic and the song list. "What's on for tonight?"

She scanned the list. "Right there," she said, pointing at Gloria Gaynor's name. "Let's get the place hopping."

The man's eyes widened. "Okay with me, sweetheart. Nail it." He turned toward the diners. "To start the evening off, we have one of Boston's own, one of our regulars — and I think she's ready to rock the house!" With a flourish, he handed the mic to her. She grasped it as though she were in a concert arena, twirled and waved at the audience.

"Ready?" Their noise assured her. She nodded at the emcee. "Let's go."

The piano chords echoed, her voice accompanied them. *I Will Survive....* And she took the crowd through the heroine's story. How the boyfriend tried to hurt her by leaving. And then the outrage of him showing up again, uninvited. But, *I Will Survive.*

It was only when she reached the end that her personal lightbulb blazed, illuminating the truth she'd hidden so well. She, too, still had a lot of love to give and to share. It flowed through her with promise and warmth. Doug Collins could no longer block the feelings she'd held frozen in place, preventing her from reaching for a full life. Only she had that power. Perhaps he'd actually done her a favor by showing up. He didn't own her heart, not anymore.

She held the mic while the crowd applauded and whistled. She didn't hear them. "What a feeling," she whispered. "I'm finally free to be...me."

##

"That was quite a performance," said Doug, quietly. "Message received, but I'll walk you home anyway. It's a long trek to Beacon Hill."

Beacon Hill? She'd moved out of her sister's home three years ago. Her decision. A big decision. But she had grown up since the tragedy, no longer that frightened sixteen-year-old girl caught in a whirlwind of anger, fear, and...grief. A girl who had searched for hope and finally the courage to spread her wings—a little bit.

She stared at Doug, who had started to leave the table, glad he was clueless. "No, thanks. I'm quite capable of making my own way."

"I know you're capable..."

"Good luck with your apartment hunting." She waved him back, headed toward the exit, then called out over her shoulder, "Why don't you try Cambridge or the Seaport?"

Her cell rang as soon as she hit the street.

"Mike! Hi—"

"Lisa's water broke," he began without preamble. "The baby's coming earlier than expected, and Emily's at a rehearsal. Can you get here right away to stay with Bobby?" His voice was tight, his words rushed. Her brother-in-law definitely did not sound like Mike Brennen, confident quarterback of the Boston Riders, a position he'd held for ten years. He sounded like a worried husband.

"Why don't you all go straight to the hospital," Jen said, "and I'll meet you there. Saves time. Seems like the baby can't wait to make an appearance."

"Great idea. See you in a few."

Walking was not an option now. Uber. She needed Uber. She searched her phone apps, made the call and paced outside the restaurant.

Five minutes could be an eternity. She barely noticed the noise when customers entered or left the place. She barely heard the karaoke music. She did recognize a familiar male voice, however, call her name.

"Jen...what are you still doing here? I thought...

"Change of plans, and look...here's my ride." She charged inside the car without waiting for driver to open her door.

"Brigham and Women's—you know where that is, right? And step on it!" She slammed the door shut and looked outside to see a puzzled Doug gazing after the cab.

Two hours later, after returning with little Bobby to her sister's house, she cuddled with her nephew, reading the three-year-old just one more story while his eyelids drifted closed. She inhaled the clean, little-boy aroma of baby shampoo and snuggled in for a goodnight kiss.

"Sweet baby," she whispered. "Your Auntie Jen loves you very much."

She heard a contented sigh, then another, and tiptoed from the room, leaving the door open. Taking one more glance, she chuckled at the sight of his nerf football under one arm and his favorite worn-out blankie under the other. At the end of the hall, she descended to the main floor of the brick Tudor, the home of her teenage and college days, the roomy suite on the top floor perfect for the adolescent girl she had been.

According to Mike, the Beacon Street house would always be home to Lisa's siblings. In time, he'd become the legal guardian along with Lisa, to Jen's younger sister and brothers. And Jen had been Lisa's right-hand gal from the beginning. Her twin brothers were still in college with two years to go, and Emily, sweet, talented

Emily, had just turned eighteen and had taken over Jen's suite.

She heard the sound of a key in the front door and glanced at her watch just as the door opened.

"Jenny! I didn't know you were coming tonight." Emily rushed forward, violin case in hand, and hugged her sister, then looked around. "Where is everyone?"

"Bobby's sleeping upstairs, maybe dreaming about his new baby sister. Come into the kitchen."

But Em's complexion had paled. "It's too soon. Isn't it?"

"Just a little. Mike said everything's fine. The baby is just…just petite." Jen pressed her lips together. "She's in an incubator, but all her systems are working. Breathing on her own. No tubes."

"Oh, that's good. Right?"

"Yeah, that's very good. She just needs time to grow. And I need you to stay home tomorrow morning with Bobby-boy. Mike'll be at the hospital with Lisa, and I have a mandatory rehearsal. The concert's in two weeks."

It seemed like a year before Emily responded. "I can change my practice time tomorrow." The teen paused, looked at Lisa with shiny eyes and quivering lips. "Why do bad things always happen in this family? Why is everything so hard? Even Lisa's little baby has…has…to struggle."

Stepping close to her sister, Jen wrapped her arms around her. "Every family has bad stuff, Em. But we Delaneys are tough. The baby, too. They're naming her Brianna. Do you know what that name means?"

Emily shook her head.

"Strong. It means strong. Brianna Grace will be as strong as we are."

"Oh-h, she has mom's name, too." With that, Emily took out her violin, and Jen knew exactly what to expect. *Amazing Grace.* The prayer her protégé sister played every night before bed to connect her to their mother.

"I'm not strong," whispered Emily, tucking the instrument under her chin. "Except when I'm playing. When I'm with Mozart, when I'm lost in that world…nothing can hurt me."

Jen's breath whooshed out, and she clasped her sister's shoulders. "You—and I—are stronger than we think, Emily. That's what I've learned. We are as strong as we need to be. Your world—even without Mozart—would be fine."

And I'm a fine one to talk. She needs Mozart like I needed Gloria Gaynor.

Emily whispered, "I can't believe that this year is my last one with the Boston Youth Symphony. I don't want it to end."

Change. Her little sister was afraid of change. Jen understood that too well.

"Oh, honey. You're heading into your next adventure is all. First, Tanglewood this summer. Didn't you say Maestro Perlman would be there again this year? Then the New England Conservatory. Come on, play for me."

Where was Mike when she needed him? Elite quarterbacks knew how to handle people. She was the worst psychologist in the world.

Emily's first note brought Jen's thoughts to a halt. No matter how often she heard her sister play, she always forgot how magnificent her music was. She recognized Mozart's *A Little Night Music.* Emily's eyes had closed, her bow flew as if of its own accord, and Jen knew the girl had, indeed, become part of another world.

She waited a bit before approaching. "Enough, Em. You need to be awake for Bobby in the morning and focus on him. Mundane, real world stuff. Got it?"

The dreamy eyes sparkled. "I think I can handle my nephew. You go to your rehearsal. No worries."

Right. In the Delaney family, there were always worries. But she wouldn't let Doug Collins be one of them. She hadn't even mentioned him to Emily, which proved her point. He was forgettable.

A few minutes before ten o'clock the next morning, Jen greeted other members of the All-City Chorus in the lobby of the Commonwealth Theater. Excitement reverberated. The group had only two full rehearsals left before their performance.

"People! People."

Jen turned toward the speaker and listened. "We've got an almost sold-out house. Our reputation is growing."

"Or we've coerced more family and friends to buy tickets!" joked one of the singers.

Jen chuckled along with the rest. Sure, family and friends would attend, but also music lovers and supporters of community talent. She loved being part of this volunteer chorus. It seemed to round out her family time and career interests. And it added to her social life. Girlfriends. Guy friends. Her days were full. Busy. No lonely moments. She made sure of that.

"Good morning, Henny-Penny."

She froze for a moment, and her heart raced. *Keep your cool, Jen.*

Pivoting slowly, she finally nodded. "Good morning, ramblin' man."

He winced. "Five years in New York. Hardly rambling."

"Depends on your outlook, I guess. Sorry, I've got to get inside and on stage with the others."

"How's Lisa doing?"

"Excuse me?" Her thoughts whirled. Nothing about the birth was in the papers today. She'd checked before leaving her apartment. Boston loved their QB, and Mike's life was public—most of the time.

"Deduction...and a hunch. I heard your directions to the driver last night. Brigham and Women's. And you were speaking with Mike." He shrugged.

"Lisa's doing just fine." And that's all she'd give him.

His expression softened. "I'm glad, Jen. Very glad."

That gentle voice, so warm and caring, reminded her of the man she used to know. Her heart ached for a moment, but she avoided his glance.

He held the heavy door open, and she walked through, feeling his eyes track her progress to the front of the theater. She joined the mezzo-sopranos on stage, all the while fighting the urge to turn around. When she couldn't postpone it a moment longer, her glance darted to the door in the back.

Gone. He was gone. She sensed her relief, then her disappointment. Now *that* was something she needed to figure out.

Lowering her gaze when she detected movement, she saw Doug settling into an aisle seat as though he had all the time in the world. What had happened to the apartment search? His work with the new play? Where were his actors? Time was money. Not that she knew where his funding came from, but still...he seemed to be wasting both time and money.

Not her business. She focused on the choral conductor and put Doug out of her mind, where he belonged.

Four-part harmonies, solos, duets— the group had worked on a variety of ways to represent the Great

American Songbook, the most enduring songs from the 1920's through the 1950's. Jen's mouth often trembled at the memories this music called up. In her mind's eye were pictures of herself singing with her mom, dad and Lisa as they cleaned up the kitchen after dinner every night. Each one could carry a mighty tune, each voice blending with the others. "Just like the Von Trapp family," her dad would offer with a grin. His eyes twinkled and his smile never faltered as the family made short work of the cleanup. A happy man.

And then...she shuddered...only the five kids remained.

Jen blinked and willed herself back to the present. Memories could still bite. She viewed the music binder in front of her, paid attention to the conductor, and allowed herself to become immersed in the practice. A full rehearsal. Corrections. Improvements. More than a hundred voices strong accompanied by a piano and small chamber group of instruments. Her jazz solo came just before intermission. *Summertime* from Porgy and Bess. By the time she took the mic, she was ready. She eyed the conductor, listened for the musical intro.

Her smoky voice gave sympathetic quality to the words, while the backup chorus added a spiritual mood. Like Emily, she could have been alone as she got lost in the music, in the emotional depth of the song and the atmosphere it evoked.

Silence followed her last note. Silence before the congrats and spontaneous applause. She was jerked from her inner world, saw and heard the approval from her peers. She'd put herself into it and knew she wouldn't be able to sing better on performance night.

Her gaze traveled to the back of the auditorium. Doug's seat was empty, but the door behind him was swinging shut. Perhaps his reappearance had sparked memories she'd carefully packed away.

His presence was getting to her. She had to admit that truth. They'd been happy together for four years. Maturing, sharing…trusting. So sweet and good. Could she have acted too hastily? She didn't know. But that was then. What she did know was that she needed to move on with her life, a full life, but a life she could control.

CHAPTER THREE

He was late. Only Jen could have made him lose track of time, place and purpose. It wasn't just her voice, it was the whole package. The girl he remembered had evolved into a woman. A woman who didn't want any part of him now.

He made his way to the management office of the theater, secured keys to the building's side door and workshop rooms he and the cast would be using, and took the stairs to the third floor. A large conference room would be fine for the initial readings. He'd meet the regional theater's creative team — producer and director — in person the next day, and auditions would begin the day after. The call had gone out, and he had a solid list of local actors to consider.

Staging a play was a cooperative venture. The most important part to Doug, however, was the play itself. The writing always was. With two successful works behind him in New York—and he still marveled at his luck— he'd now begin the intense challenge of bringing a new story to life. He couldn't be happier…professionally.

He rearranged chairs, checked electrical outlets and touched base with his director and producer. They sounded as excited as Doug. After depositing a load of pads and pens on the table, he made his way downstairs, pausing to peek into the auditorium. Jen's rehearsal was still going strong. He headed to the exit door, and almost bumped into a young woman with a little boy.

"Whoa. Sorry."

"It's okay," she said. "Come on, Bobby." She shifted the case she carried and took the child's hand.

Doug looked again. A violin case. He studied the girl. "Emily? Is that you, all grown up?"

Her brows came together, a frown appeared as she studied him. And slowly, her forehead cleared. "Oh, I recognize you. Jen's boyfriend from long ago."

Long ago. Well, in a young girl's life, five years would be a long time. "Doug Collins." He held out his hand. "You were such a little thing when I first met you. Maybe about nine years old." He felt himself pause. The child had had real problems. "How are you doing?"

Her slow smile reassured him. "Fine, but I'm running late. I hope Jen's rehearsal is over before mine begins. Hey! Does she know you're here?"

"Oh, yeah. I saw her last night, as a matter of fact."

"Really?" She turned away. "Well, I've gotta go now. C'mon, little man."

But the "little man" had thrown his nerf football down the hall and was diving in for a….

"Touchdown! Auntie Emmy, Auntie Emmy! See?"

"Oh, I see all right. Let's go find your Auntie Jen."

The boy took Emily's hand without a fuss, and Doug watched them enter the auditorium. His appointment with a Realtor was coming up, but mumbling "just five minutes," he followed them.

##

Jen heard her nephew before she saw Emily. Wasn't her sister a bit early? From her seat near the front of the theater, she waved them to her. And then she saw Doug behind them.

Darn it! Had they met already? What crummy luck. She stepped closer to greet them and swung her nephew into her arms. "Making TD's, Bobby?"

The child grinned wide enough that his six front teeth were revealed to all. "Daddy's in hop-i-tal with Mommy."

"You have a sister, Bobby. Isn't that wonderful?"

Doug chimed in next. "And you're the big brother. That little baby is lucky to have you."

Emily rolled her eyes toward Doug and gave Jen an inquiring glance.

Sighing, Jen shrugged.

"The car's outside," said Emily. "That was Mike's idea, and Luis will take me to BU's rehearsal hall. Sorry if I showed up early. I'm a bit nervous. Here's Bobby's tote bag with extra clothes and sandwiches. What time shall I tell Luis to pick you up?"

"I can't stay any longer, now that our big boy is here. I'll tell the conductor I'm leaving, but at least my solo is as good as I can get it…." Thinking out loud, she began putting words to action.

"Slow down a sec," said Doug. "I'll look after him if you don't want to leave yet."

"I'm okay with him." Jen turned toward her sister. "Tell Luis I'll find my own way home. Not to worry."

"I guess your place, since it's closer, or the house? Lisa will want to know."

Geez. "Thanks, Em." Now Doug would know where she lived. "I'll call her. Now, just go." Emily gave Bobby a kiss and left.

Jennifer faced Doug, her chin raised. "I feel like you're crowding me, Doug. You said you returned to Boston for your career. I hope that's true. I hope you're using your imagination strictly for creating your plays and not for anything else. Thanks for the offer, but I don't need you to babysit Bobby, and I don't want to go backwards. After five years…Let's just leave it alone."

His steady gaze traveled from her eyes to her nose, mouth and back. It went through her. "I can't do that," he said softly. "I've never forgotten you."

Her heart beat in syncopated rhythm like a wild tarantella. "Too late…"

"I'm not arguing now," he replied. "Go back on stage, finish the rehearsal. You know I love kids. Maybe Bobby and I will sing along."

"I can sing. 'Row, row, row the boat…'" The boy wasted no time.

It was Doug's laugh that grabbed her bruised heart. His personable, warm laughter, his easy way with her nephew. He glanced at her and winked. "Another ham in the family."

This was the Doug she remembered. Sweet. Funny. It would be so easy to pick up where they'd left off. So easy to pretend the last five years hadn't happened. Too easy. In less than twenty-four hours, he'd managed to reawaken something in her. A yearning, perhaps, that she'd refused to recognize. A yearning she'd allowed no one else to satisfy.

Too bad she didn't trust him to stick around. For a beginning playwright, New York was the place to be. Too bad also, that she needed her family as much as they needed her. Her brothers and sisters leaned on each other. They were tight, and she wasn't leaving them. She sighed deeply. Nothing was simple.

They left the theater together, and Doug apologized for needing to take off. "The house-hunt is on. So you live nearby, huh? The Downtown, area? Maybe I'll look there."

"If you can afford it. You should probably get a roommate or find a neighborhood further away. In fact, you can even go back to New York!"

"Are you kidding? After I juggled a million balls to arrange this year at BU and the theater? Besides, I can't make the single habit too easy for you."

"The-the—what?"

"I'm reaching for the gold ring, Jen. Remember this?"

His mouth covered hers, his kiss a surprise that felt so familiar, yet so new. Different. Her pulse raced, and she leaned in, enjoying the familiar sensation of his lips on hers, the familiar fragrance of his after-shave lotion before pulling back, flustered. "No, no. I-I can't go through this again."

"Neither can I, Jen." His voice sounded hoarse. "So, I'm taking a chance here, a chance on a different ending." He kissed her again, this time a quick good-bye, and left.

His words lingered in her mind—his words and her memories—as she made her way with Bobby toward Boston Common. Doug took risks all the time. He was a talented writer—she'd known that years ago—but how many writers, even brilliant ones, really earned a living? Anyone who believed that love paid the bills was a fool. Now where had that thought come from? She'd never been curious about the financial side of him. She'd only noticed the talent side.

What was he really doing back in Beantown? That kiss…tears started to run down her face. "Damn, damn, damn…and just when I had it all figured out."

She and Bobby watched the swan boats, played catch, and ran after the football. She called Lisa for a medical update on her and her new daughter and was relieved at her sister's calm words. The afternoon turned to early evening by the time Jen returned Bobby to his dad—a dad they found sound asleep on the living room couch.

"Shh…" warned Jen with a finger on her lips. "Just give a gentle hug. Let him sleep."

"Dad-dy!!"

Mike rolled over, grabbed his son, and bestowed dozens of kisses on the boy's neck and belly. Giggles ensued before the man stood, child in his arms, and looked at Jennifer.

"Thanks for taking him, Jenny. After two bad experiences, I don't think Lisa will ever agree to another nanny. My folks are driving in tomorrow, but you have been a lifesaver. Don't know what we'd do without you."

Jen shrugged. "No worries, Mike. I'm not going anywhere. Families take care of each other, don't they? Just like you and Lisa took care of us." The past seemed to haunt her today, and unexpectedly, her lips began to tremble. Pressing them hard together, she tried to divert Mike. "Uh — tell me all about the baby."

He grabbed the bait, and for the next five minutes, she heard all about the perfect, but miniature Brianna Grace Brennan. "I swear, she's no bigger than a football."

"I'll run to the hospital for a quick visit and then head home," she said. "You okay with Bobby?"

"Of course. Right, son?"

They high-fived each other. "I played ball with a big man today. Auntie Jen was singing, and I played."

Mike's quizzical gaze found her, and Jen sighed. "Okay. Emily would have mentioned it anyway." She looked him in the eye. "Doug Collins moved back—he's teaching at BU and putting on a play at the Commonwealth— and the first thing he did was track me down, and I don't know how I feel about it because I'm afraid…I'm afraid…." She felt tears well and pushed them away. "I'm afraid to get involved again, and that's all I know for now. I'm an idiot for even talking to him."

She stepped toward the hallway. Mike's voice followed her. "I used to like the guy. But not at your expense. Want me to pay him a visit?"

"Oh, God, no!" she replied, twirling toward him again. "I'm a big girl now, Mike. I'll handle it."

"Sometimes, honey, an interception's in order. At other times, getting to the end zone simply takes a lot of running plays, a lot of zig-zagging."

She inhaled. "I get it. But you can't reach the end zone if you don't trust your players."

CHAPTER FOUR

Doug signed a one-year lease for a studio apartment on Devonshire Street, in the downtown area of the city. It might or might not be near Jennifer's place—he had no idea exactly where she lived but was content with his choice. Not far from both the theater and university.

On Sunday morning, Evie had stopped by as he unloaded his clothes, computer and books from his car, making several trips inside with his arms full. It was good to have his own place again, and even though his sister's hug had felt extra-strong a little while ago, he was sure she felt the same. In her scrubs and white jacket, she'd looked every inch a physician.

"The folks are very proud of you, Eve. I can just hear Dad saying 'my daughter, the doctor.'" His grin was warm with his own pride.

She shrugged. "I suppose. But I just wish—" She shook her head.

"Forget it, Evie. He's not going to boast about his son, the writer. Been there, done that, with our parental units. I'm over it."

"But you're so smart. Your work is so good. A full-length play and a one-act on Broadway, and now you're here with something new to work on. I just don't understand them, and I'm sorry."

He wrapped his younger sister in his arms. "It doesn't matter. Writing is who I am. Sometimes, getting it exactly right drives me nuts, but... in the end, I love it."

Her smile reassured him. "I love my work too," Eve said. "Not so crazy about the hours, though."

"It's the love part that counts more. Trust me. If you're going to spend your whole life doing something, be sure it makes you happy."

"Good advice, Doug. I'm so glad you're back." She gave him a quick kiss and left for the hospital.

He could have done worse than having Eve as a sister. They'd forged a better relationship since they'd grown up and moved away from home. He hung up the last of his shirts and ran down the two flights to the ground floor, out the front door of the building and smack into Jennifer Delaney.

"Wow. How lucky can one man get? Do you actually live in this building?"

"You're not *that* lucky, kiddo. I'm up about two blocks, but you've got a great coffee shop on your corner." She held up her large to-go cup and continued to walk.

"No time for a friend?"

"I've got a busy day."

"Will every day be too busy for us?"

That stopped her. She turned slowly toward him, her brow furrowed, eyes shadowed. "There is no 'us' anymore. You were gone for a long time."

"It was a five-year residency, Jen."

She nodded. "Five years in two separate worlds. I know circumstances were lousy, but life went on, and we owe each other nothing. Couples break up every day. Let's say we each had a clean slate after the visits stopped and phone calls became fewer. A clean slate after you were gone for a while.

"Figured it all out, huh? As easy as that." He snapped his fingers.

"I didn't say it was easy," she protested. "But I'm not going backward."

He could live with that. But she'd given him an opening that he wasn't going to ignore. "Then how about starting over? As you said, the slate's clean."

##

Whew! If he weren't so sincere—and cute—at the same time. If his eyes didn't implore, if he didn't sound as though the future of civilization depended on her response.... And his mouth—she loved his mouth.

"My imagination isn't as good as yours. I can't simply forget the past."

"Then put it in a box on a high closet shelf out of the way. Examine it from time to time if you have to, but don't let it be a barricade now."

What a picture. "I keep forgetting…"

"Forgetting what?"

"…how good you are with words."

"Normally, I'd say thanks. But somehow, I'm not taking that as a compliment right now."

Her building was just ahead, and she glanced at her watch. "I want to visit Lisa and the baby. Then hit the books."

"Going for an MBA?"

"Already have it. But I've got in-house training this week and want to be prepared. My career means a lot to me, and I don't want to screw it up."

His eyes shone, and a grin appeared. "Henny-Penny, I've always had full confidence in you and still do. You are one smart lady, and I'm sure you'll be fully prepared.'"

Startled, she stepped back. "Thanks, I guess. But I don't take anything for granted. I've worked hard. Frankly, I'm terrified of failing."

She heard his "whoa," and then silence settled around them.

"Terrified is a strong word," said Doug.

"A true word. I want to make my parents proud of me."

"I think," Doug said slowly, "that might be overkill."

"Why?" she asked, her voice rising in defense. "Because they're gone?"

"Not at all." He stepped closer and framed her face in his hands. "I'm twenty-eight years old and have two shows running in New York at the same time. That's rare—very rare—and my folks could care less. So, what does their approval mean in the end? Nothing. You go after your dreams because inside, you know it's the right path."

"I like numbers," she whispered. "Always have. And that liking morphed into a dream career with a world-renowned investment firm."

"I know. And numbers give me a rash."

She smiled. He'd always been able to make her laugh. Seemed he still could. And maybe that was not a small thing.

"You know what gave me a rash in the old days?" she asked.

"Of course, I do. Writing those personal essays. The insult of revealing your thoughts and feelings to a bunch of strangers. I'll never forget the fire in your eyes when you stalked toward that door, ready to quit the class."

"But I needed those three credits to get my degree." Her voice fell away as the memory played as sharply as if it had happened yesterday. "The essays were all submitted anonymously. The prof picked you to read mine. And when I reached the door—my hand was on the knob— you said I couldn't leave, that the course was required for graduation. Smarty-pants." But a shard of pain still stung inside.

"Maybe...just maybe," Doug slowly began, "it was too soon for you to take that writing course."

She stared at him then, examining his features, discerning a softness, a compassion that she hadn't noticed then.

"Who knows?" she replied, her voice low. "That shrink all us kids visited after the accident wanted us to write in a diary. A private journal..." She shrugged. "That class lasted for one semester—the longest ever fifteen weeks in college—but in the end, I handled it."

She watched him pull out his phone. "You handled that and a lot of other things. Now, can you handle giving me your cell number? Or will I have to call you at work and interrupt you again and again?"

"Fools rush in..." she sang quietly.

His head jerked up. "You won't be sorry, Jenny. We'll take it slow."

Maybe it was the only way to discover once and for all what it was about this man that put other men in the shade. She'd spent five years keeping busier than ten people so as not to miss him. *I Will Survive.* As the song had reminded her Friday night, she had a lot of love to give. If Doug had frozen her heart, then maybe he was the right one to melt it again or at least help her reach a closure that worked. A final closure. So she'd be able to move on.

"It's not the speed," she whispered. "It's the uncertainty. The trust." She extended her hand. "Give me your phone."

##

Trust was a big one. *The only one.* Doug couldn't get the word out of his mind all day as he finished setting up his apartment, made and answered phone calls, and once more studied the script for *The Sanctuary.* Jen had a trust problem with him. Of course, she was wrong. He'd never hurt her. Never. In time, she'd understand that.

Back in the theater on Monday morning, Doug greeted the play's producer, who had many projects behind him, and the young director, who'd already made a name for herself locally. They wore big smiles, and exuded high energy and anticipation. A great way to start.

"I'm thrilled that you've decided to stage this in Boston," said Lynn, as she shook Doug's hand and sat down. She glanced at her cohort. "We both are."

"You won't be sorry," added Jake. "Our theater group has won many awards due to our high-quality performances, provided, I might add, at a fair price."

"Two excellent attributes for a successful playhouse," said Doug with a smile. "Since I'm on staff at the university this year, I'd say it all worked out." He held up his well-worn script. "Can we get down to business now?"

Instantly, the conversation ceased, and the analysis began. Doug noted that each of the others' manuscripts looked as dog-eared as his. Theater was a risky business, and no one wanted to fail.

Three hours went by before Doug's stomach growled. He looked at his watch and pushed his chair back. "I'm starving."

But he felt Lynn's hand on his arm. "Before we break, I just want to say how much I love this play. I love each character. And I love the title. *The Sanctuary.* It's perfect."

"Thanks," said Doug. "It's funny how sometimes a title comes hard, but this one...? It whispered to me."

"It's a winner all around," confirmed Jake. "The way I see it, our mission is to cast it properly here, have a good run, and then you can bring it to New York."

Doug's stomach tightened. "Let's take one step at a time." Sure, Broadway was the goal, but as he'd told Jen, he'd just be a consultant and commute to New York as needed. "We'll see what happens."

He watched the other two exchange a quizzical glance. "We'll see?" asked Lynn. "There's no 'we'll see' about it. This is a powerful story. It deserves to be on Broadway!"

Doug cocked his head and smiled appreciatively. "Nice to have a fan club, but let's just say, I'm paying it forward. My first play, *The Broken Circle,* was produced here when I was a lowly undergrad, and now it's doing well in New York." He shook his head. "Sometimes I can hardly believe it myself."

But his success had come with a price. A vision of Jen filled his mind—Jen in all her moods – thoughtful, with a crinkle in her brow, happy, with a wide, beautiful smile, loving, with a warmth in her eyes and gentle hands caressing his cheek. He'd turned his world upside down because of her, always knew he would after he'd tied up his loose ends in New York. Their story was not yet finished.

##

So much for giving him my cell number. At ten that evening, after a full day of client meetings followed by the training seminar, Jen yawned and prepared for bed. She hadn't heard from Doug all day, and the flash of disappointment she felt annoyed her.

But just then she heard the whoosh of a text signal. She glanced at her phone and felt herself smile.

R U up?

Big day. Just about to go to bed.

Not yet.

The phone rang. "So how did your busy day go?"

"Hang on. I want to get comfortable." She leaned back against her pillows before replying. "Actually, my day went very well both personally and professionally. Lisa's home, and if all goes well, baby Brianna should be home in a few days."

"That's really great. A load off your mind—off everyone's mind—knowing how close your family is."

His last sentence echoed the past. "Nothing's changed about that, Doug." Her voice hardened. "The Delaney-Brennan clan is tight. Always will be. So, if that's still a problem for you…?"

"Holy Toledo, Jen! Take a breath. Cool it."

She waited.

He spoke again, his tone calm. "Of course, I know your family's tight. And I know you all had to be in order to survive. Okay? And now, you're all grown up, living a grown-up life."

"Still in Boston."

She heard his laugh. "So you are. And here I am, back here, too."

Her muscles relaxed one by one, like a balloon slowly deflating. "I guess so. At least, you seem to be—for now."

"Count on it, Jenny. I'm not going anywhere. Now, tell me about your great day in the office."

Okay, he was trying. "Lots of training with more to come. All part of growing my career."

"So what do you actually do?"

She paused, wondered if he'd get it. "Simply put, I help clients plan for their financial future. You know— the usual. Investment guidance, retirement planning, income strategies, wealth management and even college planning. I've got my Series 7 and 63 as well as my insurance licenses. I love doing this."

A low whistle came through the line. "All that from the girl who computed the family budget and told her big sister how much to spend?"

"Lisa couldn't even balance a checkbook back then. I figured it out at sixteen. And why do you remember that little factoid?"

"Henny-Penny, there isn't anything about you that I don't remember."

Her breath caught. "Sounds scary."

"Nope. Sounds like I'm getting your attention."

Time to change the subject. "And how was *your* day?"

"Want the good news first, or the bad news?"

"Bad news? Already? You just started. I swear, a career like yours would give me hives."

"And the stock market doesn't go up and down?"

"We plan for that. We plan for all the contingencies."

His quiet laughter came through the phone. "What a big word! Contingencies. Sounds to me that it's more about control. Sweetheart, no matter how hard you work, you can't control the world."

"But I sure as shootin' can control *my* world."

##

It was the way she said it, so seriously, as if she truly had total power, that amused him as he said goodnight. Her tender spot. Her world had exploded years ago but would never do so again—if Jen had anything to say about it.

When his phone rang, he saw Jen's name and answered quickly.

"Anything wrong?"

"We talked about *my* job, but you didn't tell me about your day."

A soft and sexy voice. No wonder she was a natural jazz singer.

"You're right. So…"

"Good news first," she interrupted. "Let me enjoy it before problems rear their nasty heads."

"Not your problems to solve, kiddo. I've got this."

Silence met his ear. "Jen? Still there?"

"Y-e-s." She sounded unsure.

"What?"

"Just thinking. You're right. I don't have to solve your problems. You're an adult now, too. With one show on Broadway, and one off-Broadway, you must be earning a living. So, tell me the good news."

"The producer and director for *The Sanctuary* love the script, which means they'll go to hell and back to do it right. Tomorrow, we're holding our first auditions for the main characters. It's an exciting time. And I'm betting on Boston not to let me down." She'd never understand the chance he was taking by leaving New York.

"It won't. Just like when *The Broken Circle* was put on in school. It was— was like magic. You almost cried."

"You were supposed to forget about that!"

"Nah. I could see you were overwhelmed. Awestruck to see your printed words brought to life." She paused, and he waited. "Doug?"

"Yeah?"

"Is it still like that? Still awesome?"

"Every. Single. Time."

She spoke softly then. So softly, he strained to hear her. "Then I guess you made the right choice five years ago...and for the right reasons."

He couldn't breathe.

"And so did I," she whispered.

LINDA BARRETT

CHAPTER FIVE

It was hard to put Doug out of her mind, to pretend he wasn't back in town. That idea was totally unrealistic now. After a restless night, however, Jen went to work the next day determined to keep a friendly distance. Doug could be one of her guy friends. Like Evan or Matt. She and Doug had both found what they'd been seeking. They'd put their educations to good use. He loved his work, she loved hers. Correct choices. Case closed. The past was in the past.

Within five minutes at work, she was fully engrossed—personal appointments, customer calls, and her own seminar that afternoon. At quitting time, she grabbed her purse and realized she'd gotten through the day without thinking about Doug too much, if she didn't count every in-between moment. He was someone she used to know…as the song said.

Her cell rang at ten o'clock that evening.

"How was your day?" came the familiar voice.

"Busy. As is the rest of my week."

"Ouch. Sending me a message?"

Was she? "I'm…figuring that out myself."

"Take all the time you need. I'm not going anywhere."

That seemed to be his theme. Time to focus on him. "And how was *your* day?"

"My day…well, as it happens, I have good news and bad news."

"Again? That seems to be your daily report. I do not like bad news, not anyone's bad news." Her throat began closing, her voice quiet. Even ten years later, the words instilled fear.

"Jenny, shh…not to worry. It's professional, not personal."

Didn't matter. Her adrenaline surged anyway. Bad news meant all her senses on alert. "Okay, I'm ready."

"I heard from my agent friend today. I'd sent him a novel a month ago."

"A novel? You mean a regular story—a book—and not a play?"

"Yeah."

"He didn't like it? That's so hard to believe. You come up with such powerful ideas…powerful work."

"Oh, he loved the storyline."

"But…?"

"Said it should have been a play. Seventy percent of the book was dialogue. And the other thirty, he said, sounded like I was bossing everyone around. Sitting, standing, shoving."

Jen started to laugh, then giggle. "Huh! Guess that big playwriting residency didn't make much of an impression on you. The first time you're on your own, you choose to write a novel! A novel that's really a play.

Too funny, Doug, weird and funny. I guess you are who you are."

He sighed dramatically. "I think you're right. But it was worth the effort just to hear you laugh. Love that laugh."

Too personal. "So what are you going to do with that story now?"

"Isn't it obvious? I'm going to take my friend's advice and rewrite it. Writing is rewriting most of the time anyway."

"With your other jobs, it sounds like you'll be busy twenty-four seven. Maybe that's best — for both of us." She couldn't deny the feelings he'd reawakened in her, but she wasn't ready. Time and space suited her. "I'll say goodnight now." She disconnected.

Not a second later she heard a ding. A text from the failed novelist. *"Sorry to spoil your plan, Jenny. On my To-Do list, you are Number One."*

#

"Didn't Lisa tell you?" asked Mike over the phone.

"I guess not."

"Luis is picking up the boys at the airport tomorrow and bringing them home. You're off the hook for once."

Mike's driver was like part of the family, but not usually around too much in the off-season. "Then I'll meet you at the house," said Jen. "I want to see my brothers."

"That's up to you. But you're screwing up a Friday night...uh...with your friends."

"What?"

"Go out. Have fun."

Since when…? "What's this all about? I'm with my friends often enough. You're talking to good old Jenny here. And you do not sound like good old Mike."

"Big-brother Mike is talking now. You need to have more fun. And the Brennan-Delaney clan is not going to screw it up for you this time around."

She sucked back both her tears and laughter. Her thoughts swirled. This time around? Could they know the real reason she stayed five years ago? She'd made a strong effort hide her pain and confusion. Even Lisa hadn't asked too many questions—just accepted that Doug needed to be in New York. And maybe, with all that was happening between her and Mike at the time, she preferred Jen at home, too.

"But you're all my family!" Jen protested. "Nothing's more important. You're doing Lisa's dirty work, aren't you? She's behind this ridiculous conversation."

"If it's dirty work, then we're both involved—Lisa and I."

"I-I don't understand, but I'm not going to make a fuss now. You guys still have a full house to handle, including an itty-bitty baby and a three-year-old." She thought about the twins, and Emily's concert on Saturday, plus Lisa and Mike's careers. Lisa's legal practice needed her hands-on involvement. It was a lot. "If it will make you both happier to think I'm…socializing, then fine. But this conversation is not over."

"Agreed. And one more thing, Jen. Bring Doug to visit us whenever you want."

Doug. *Now* she clearly understood the motivation behind this discussion. First up, though, she needed to change the mood. "You and Lisa can take off your hair shirts," she said. "The past is all on me."

##

On Friday evening, Jen made her way to the lobby of her office building to meet her friends and spotted Doug among them. She didn't recall inviting him, but wasn't too surprised. He'd felt welcomed the week before and "people-person" Doug probably assumed he was now part of the group.

A wide smile lit up his face when she approached, and she felt herself smile back, her doubts beginning to dissolve as she was drawn to his warmth. He hurried toward her and wasted no time planting a kiss on her mouth—as though he had the right.

"Slow down, cowboy. You're way ahead of me."

"I always was...always circled back to let you catch up."

Was that true? "Tortoise and the hare?" she joked. She'd think about the implications later.

"Didn't matter," he replied, "since we were heading in the same direction." He paused, his brown eyes darkening, turning solemn. "It seems I've circled back again."

"Your choice," she whispered, avoiding his gaze.

"Hey, Jennifer!" She glanced up to see Alexis and Liz waving.

"A lucky save," said Doug, smiling at the newcomers. "Where's the rest of the crew?"

"Evan's coming." said Alexis, "but Matt said he'd catch up at Maguire's." She turned toward Liz. "Do you know what's holding him up on a Friday night?"

Liz glanced away. "Just working late, I guess."

"Hmm..." Jen glanced at Alexis, who shrugged.

Another elevator deposited its passengers. "There's Evan. Let's go. I'm starving." Doug's stomach growled in time to his words. "It keeps doing that," he joked.

"Because you're always starving," said Jen. She sighed dramatically. "Whether it's poets, playwrights, writers....starving seems to be the keyword."

Doug rolled his eyes and opened the outside door. "Spare me, will ya'? In fact, I had a terrific day." He grinned at them. "The auditions were great, and we're all cast. Full reading starts Monday."

"Hear, hear! I'm impressed," said Evan. "Maybe I pegged you wrong. That's quite an achievement in one week."

"Sure was fast. You really are the hare," commented Jen.

"Don't you business types always say 'time is money?' " asked Doug. "We've got the main stage booked for the second weekend of September and for eight weekends thereafter, plus Wednesdays. We'd better be ready."

"I can't wait to see it," said Alexis. "I've never known a real playwright. Or any writer, in fact."

They'd arrived at Maguire's as Liz said, "Let's make it a party. An opening-night party. All of us."

"We'll see," said Jen. Four months from then seemed like an eternity. Who knew what her relationship with Doug would be? She glanced at him and received a wink. "You'll be there," he whispered, "and I hope you'll be cheering."

"I can't make promises I may not keep."

She heard his deep inhale and exhale. "Maybe you're right. Let's find out." He leaned forward, his arms around her, and placed his mouth on hers. Gentle at first, then pressing harder, and she opened to him, her tongue meeting his. Her eyes closed, her breath disappeared as she absorbed his familiar touch, his familiar fragrance. Comforting, secure...exciting. A frisson of happiness raced through her as time disappeared.

Her friends cheered, and reality brought her up short.

"Oh, man…" she turned aside, her face on fire. Public displays of affection were definitely not her style.

"I'm not asking for promises," said Doug, keeping her close. "Take your time." But his grin belied his words. He leaned closer and whispered, "Nothing has changed since our undergrad days. You're still the one. And so am I."

"And that's supposed to make me happy?" she whispered, glad to see Evan pointing at a table.

"C'mon, lovebirds," the man said, leading the way. "The crowd's lighter than last week. I guess people are grabbing weekends at the Cape already."

Lovebirds? She'd have to straighten Evan out.

"I'd love a place on Cape Cod," said Alexis. "The beach, the ocean… Work hard, play hard."

Jen sat quietly, her mind flashing to the large beach house Mike had bought several years ago for the family to enjoy. Their summer neighbors had come to accept him as just another resident, regardless of the three Super Bowls he'd led the Riders to win. But as usual, she didn't share details of her home life, even with these closest friends. Her family's past experiences with paparazzi and their invasive techniques precluded that.

"Oh, here's Matt," exclaimed Liz, her body poised to stand—or fly. Jen eyed Alexis and nodded toward their friend. Alexis shook her head and seemed confused.

Matt approached, but his gaze was only for Liz. "It's what we thought." He turned to include the table. "I've got some news," he began. "I'm being promoted." He held up his hand to stop Jen as she began to congratulate him. "All those late-night courses seemed to have paid off. However, there's a kink." He looked from one to the other. "The new position requires me to relocate to a regional office."

Alexis was the first. "Congratulations...I think. But we'll miss you, Matt. Oh, I'm not ready for this. I wasn't expecting my little working world to fall apart."

"Did you think this—" Evan gestured around the table "—could last forever?"

"I-I guess I never thought about it," said Alexis. "But why not? The Boston office is huge. It's the corporate headquarters. I thought we'd all be together for years."

"So did I," admitted Jen, blinking quickly.

Doug remained silent, but Jen sensed him staring at her and her co-workers, taking it all in. Fodder for another play?

"So, exactly where are you going, Matt?" she asked softly. "Maybe just to Rhode Island?"

Matt cleared his throat. "Actually, I'll be further away than that—in Kentucky. Working at the office in Covington."

"That's far!" Jen cried, her stomach twisting. "That's a real goodbye."

"Haven't you heard of planes?" joked Evan.

"Not the same," she protested. "Nothing ever stays the same." She heard the cry in her own voice and pressed her lips together.

"Jenny—look at me," said Doug, gently turning her head. "Think of it not as a goodbye but as a hello—for Matt. New challenges, building his career. That's what you all want, isn't it? And sometimes moving is what's required."

He wasn't talking only about Matt. He was speaking about them. About their past when moving to New York City was out of the question—for her. It still was.

Liz's quiet voice broke in. "He won't be going alone."

All eyes turned to her. "We're going together. Hopefully, I'll work something out with the company. If not, I'll go job hunting."

Matt stood behind Liz, his hands resting on her shoulders. He leaned over and kissed her on the cheek before addressing the group.

"You would have figured this out soon, but Lizzy and I—we've been seeing each other away from the office for almost a year now....And, well...we're taking the relationship to the next level." He smiled. "More news to follow."

"A toast to your new adventure," said Doug, raising his water glass.

"Yes. Of-of course," said Jen, pasting a smile on her face while in the back of her mind, Carol King asked if anybody stayed in one place anymore.

##

"We're bringing the baby home today."

Jen sat on the side of her bed the next morning, her sister's words floating above her as she held her phone and tried to wake up. The message, when received, had her bolting from the pillow. "That's wonderful. I can't wait to see her again."

"Neither can I. But I need a favor. Instead of meeting us, can you accompany Emily to Symphony Hall tonight?"

Emily's concert. A very big deal. "Of course."

"I...I feel awful not going with her, but Brianna needs me, too."

"She certainly does! Don't think twice about it. Emily can even stay overnight at my place."

"Thanks, but she'll probably want to come home. She's funny that way. Can't wait to get to school, but—and this worries me—she's happiest when she's alone and practicing her violin."

Nothing new there. "Lis—she's just being herself. And she's so good with that fiddle. Practicing is a one-person job."

"I know, I know. But I'm not sure. Heck, I'm not sure of anything. Maybe my hormones are out of whack now. Sometimes I wonder if Emily still thinks Mom can hear her in heaven? Is that why she's relentless with her playing? She's not seven years old anymore!"

Goosebumps popped up on Jen's skin. "She can't believe that now." A kaleidoscope of family memories invaded her mind, finally bringing her to the prior night's conversation at Maguire's.

"Maybe we're all carrying around a piece of the past," she said softly. "You, me, Em, our brothers. Maybe it doesn't go away, and we just deal with it the best we can."

A long, low whistle came through the phone. "Quite the philosopher so early in the morning."

Jen chuckled. "I try." But did she? For the first time in a long time, she wasn't sure.

"Mike and I don't worry about you anymore. You figured out what you wanted and never looked back."

Maybe, where Doug was concerned. "Thanks, but it was a no-brainer. Finance and I are a natural fit."

"Don't I know it! Oh...Bobby's calling me. See you later."

A natural fit, Jen thought, as she disconnected. For the first time in her adult life, she wondered if her career was enough. Her family? Friends? Her choral group? She'd never questioned her choices. But since Doug had reappeared only a week ago, he'd turned her life into one big question mark.

CHAPTER SIX

Friday night with Jen and her friends wasn't enough. His
nightly phone calls to her were good, but not good
enough either. He wanted more. He needed more. On
Saturday morning, Doug started a small pot of coffee
and glanced at his calendar. Every box was filling up.
The new play required not only rehearsals but meetings
with Jake about publicity and community sponsors. He
had to prepare for the new semester at BU. He had ideas
for his advanced students that he wanted to implement
himself. And of course, a revision to *Straight from the
Heart*. All important goals, but not more important than
his first priority: Jen.

He poured the coffee into his mug and sipped. He
wanted to build his relationship with her. Built it slowly,
with trust. Court her! He smiled, first, at his old-
fashioned word choice, and second, because he realized
that "courting" was essentially what the hero of his

novel had decided to do while searching for his ending. Not too surprising when he'd based the heroine on Jen.

Picking up his cell, he pressed her number.

"Hey, Doug. I'm just out of the shower. Can I call you back?"

Shower? Images of a glorious, naked Jen bombarded him, with her long legs, soft breasts—but he bit his tongue. "Absolutely. I'll be...ah...waiting." *Dreaming.*

But just as Friday nights and nightly calls weren't enough, dreaming wasn't enough either. He answered the phone on the first ring. "It's Saturday," he said. "Let's spend the day together. Wherever you want to go. Whatever you want to do. I can pick you up in thirty minutes."

Silence. Then, "I'm sorry, Doug. The twins are back, and Emily's got her concert tonight. Little Brianna's coming home today too. I'm really busy...and—and...well you know the routine with my family. Everything's happening at once."

"I'll take you and Emily to the concert tonight," he responded.

"You haven't heard anything I just said."

"I'm ignoring it. While I'd really like to spend the entire day with you, I'm also trying to show some understanding. Don't I get points for that?"

He heard a reluctant laugh and smiled. Humor. Humor always worked.

"You'd need a ticket for tonight. The concert's at Symphony Hall, a really big deal, and Emily...well, she might be as highly strung as her violin. Uh...that's a family joke...sort of."

"Very funny. I'm glad you shared it. And don't be sorry when you realize what you said." Sharing a *family* joke was a good sign—almost like in the old days.

"I'm sorry already. See you at five o'clock. At the house."

"I'll be there."

He hung up and wanted to cheer. Better than sharing that joke, she'd just invited him to her most precious place. A place he hadn't entered in five years. Her family's home. That was the upside. The downside? How would he be received?

Shrugging, he searched for the Symphony Hall website. He couldn't control how Jen's siblings felt about him reappearing, but he could buy a last-minute ticket to Emily's concert.

Doug immediately spotted the limousine as he approached the house on Beacon Street. He shouldn't have been surprised. Mike Brennan would make sure Emily's special night was special in all ways. And safe, too. He had to admit the guy had taken on a load of responsibility when he'd married his wife.

Doug had liked the man when they'd first met. After learning Doug was a writer, Mike had extended his hand, saying "Welcome to my world, Doug, where you either have what it takes or you don't."

"Thanks. I intend to make my own kind of touchdowns."

He recalled that conversation and stood a little taller as he approached the door. Whatever his reception, Jen was worth it.

The door swung wide before he could knock. And there stood Jennifer Grace Delaney. Stunning. Long sparkly earrings, a black dress that hugged her figure and strappy, high-heeled sandals. The woman had legs. Did she ever. He took it all in with a glance and then focused on her eyes. Her violet eyes shone, then darkened as she looked up at him.

"You clean up pretty well, Doug…."

His reservations melted as he burst into laughter. "Glad you approve. I did learn a little something in New York."

"Well, come in, come in." She stepped back, and he walked into familiar territory—with a twist. No one matched his memories in the small crowd that had gathered. Two identical-looking young men approached him, same blonde hair, green eyes, same walk and body movement. Dressed up for a night out.

"There's no way I can distinguish between you two," Doug said, extending his hand. "But it's amazing to see the grown-up version of the boys I once knew."

"We're not done growing yet, I hope," said one, his voice light. "I'm Brian."

"But we're old enough now to figure things out." This brother's tone was more serious. "I'm Andy. And, if you haven't noticed, we're both going with you and Jen to the concert."

"We couldn't disappoint Emily," added his brother, with a meaningful glance back at his twin.

The air had definitely cooled. He had walked into the proverbial lion's den.

"For crying out loud," said Jen. "Cut the drama. Doug's an old friend. Just a friend. So relax and focus on your little sister."

"But we…"

"You were sad…"

"I can take care of myself, boys," said Jen. "Stick to baseball."

"Mike's not liking…"

She turned to Doug then. "If you want to change your mind about going, I'll understand. Maybe there's such a thing as too much family!"

"I wish mine were more like yours." His unplanned response surprised him. And must have surprised Jen, from the wide-eyed look on her face.

"I never knew that."

"I didn't either. Until this minute. But I have a great sister."

She flashed a warm smile. "I remember. Sisters are the best. And speaking of..." She nodded toward the hallway.

Emily appeared. White blouse, long black skirt. Violin case in her hand. "We need to go," she said quietly. "Lisa and Mike are with the baby. And Bobby won't leave their side. So let's just go."

"You're the boss tonight," said Jen, her arm going around the girl.

"I always think Mozart is my boss or Mendelson but then...when I play, I think maybe it's me who's the boss. You know, it's complicated."

Doug caught the questioning look passing between the brothers. "The limo's outside," he said quickly. "Are you ready, Jen?"

She nodded. "C'mon, everyone."

Luis stood by the car and waved them in. "Now we've got the whole family back. Mr. Brennan likes summertime the best."

"So do I," said Jen, as she entered the car after Emily. "Even if my bros drive me a bit crazy."

But Doug could see the love for them in her laughing eyes as she teased. A good big sister, and he'd bet the boys counted on her. Or took her for granted. He was in no position to ask questions, but maybe he could do a good turn for Jen's little sister.

"Hey, Emily, you got me thinking about what you said about Mozart. I feel like that too. Sometimes, I get lost in my writing. Sometimes, I don't know where the words come from. Is Mozart your boss? Or does his music carry you away, until you're lost and just play it from your heart? You're right about it being complicated—especially when you're really talented like you—but it's also very satisfying."

"Yes," said Emily. "It just feels...good!"

"Mike's his own boss," said Brian. "And the team leader. He keeps practicing until he's better than anyone."

"He loves the game," said Andy slowly. "In all ways—heart, mind and body. He calls the plays, but he's also part of the team. When you think about it, everything really is complicated."

"Even Mike can't play such a tough game forever," said Emily slowly. "But I want to make music forever."

They were quiet for the few more minutes it took Luis to reach their destination. When the car slowed to a stop, Doug looked out the window. "We're here."

"Wow, I didn't have time to be nervous," said Emily, "until right now. Good conversation."

Luis opened the door and they scrambled out, each thanking the man. Emily led the way. "I have to use the side door, but I'll see you later."

"Good luck." Jen hugged her. "We love you no matter what."

"Yeah, just don't throw up," said Brian.

"Like you used to," added Andy.

She rolled her eyes. "They never forget anything!"

"As we theater-people say," said Doug, "break a leg."

Emily grinned and disappeared into the building.

"Whew," said Jen. "We did it. It took all of us, but we did it." She glanced at him. "Thanks for distracting her with that conversation." Then she gathered her brothers, one on each arm. "Love having you both back from school."

Doug saw it on her face, heard it in her voice. When she loved, she loved hard. And he wanted that.

She stared at him then, head tilted, eyes bright. "Now, do you understand?" she asked quietly.

"I do understand. And if that was the whole point of today's visit, then you've wasted your time. I'm not in competition with your family. But you have to figure that out."

##

After the concert, Luis took Emily and the twins home, and dropped Jen and Doug downtown. As they started walking toward their apartments, Jen found her hand resting in Doug's, as though it were the most natural place to be. Had Doug been right earlier? Had she wanted him to see how close her family was so…so she didn't have to feel guilty about the past anymore? *Oh, yeah, Jen. Still trying to prove you were right?*

"Emily was amazing, wasn't she?" Jen said.

"I'd say. Standing-ovation kind of amazing. I had no idea she'd be a featured player. A major one."

"She's going to Tanglewood in a couple of weeks," Jen said, "the summer home of the Boston Symphony. She might be the youngest there, only eighteen and playing with the best. She used to spend summers at a music camp run by Itzhak Perlman and his wife. She had to audition to get accepted."

Doug's long, low whistle reassured her.

"Tanglewood's across the state," she said, "and I'll probably drive her. Emily doesn't have a license yet— it's never even come up in conversation!" She shook her head and sighed. "I swear she lives in the clouds. The girl needs a keeper! But I can't see Mike leaving Lisa and the kids to chauffeur her. And Luis has a vacation planned. So, I'll go."

"Want company? I grew up nearby and know exactly where it is."

She needed to think. "Will you turn it into a family visit as well?" Funny that she'd never met his parents during their four years of undergrad school. They lived far away, and she hadn't thought too much about it then. But now she wondered.

"Probably not."

"Axe murderers?"

He laughed, his eyes gleaming. "Not quite that bad, but not up to your standards. Or mine, either, for that matter."

She stopped walking. "My standards? I'd never judge them."

"Oh, yes, you would, but it doesn't matter." He faced her then, took her head gently between his hands. "*They* don't matter. This is about you and me. Not the extra players on the set. Because in the end, when you go to sleep at night, only one person will be sharing your pillow."

Her breath caught on the truth of his words. Only one person...or, it seemed, no one.

He leaned over and touched his mouth to her lips. One touch, and whatever fire she'd tamped down through the years blazed again. She kissed him with a hunger that surprised her. Stunned her. But filled her with well-being.

His embrace tightened. "Jen?" He pointed at her building. "You know how I feel about you, but it's your call."

My call. Only a man who cared for her—perhaps really loved her—would toss that ball into her court. Living in limbo had to end. It seemed she'd put her life on hold for five long years. "Maybe I've been waiting...all this time," she whispered, as she took his hand and led him inside. Together, they ran up the one flight to her door. And to her bed.

##

The right decision. Afterward, amid the tossed blankets and clothes, amid the renewed and new knowledge of one another, Jen cuddled next to him, one arm around his waist while his lay around hers. "So glad you came back," she murmured, "home to Boston, home to me."

"Home," he sighed. "A simple word that's sometimes not so simple."

"It is now. You're here."

He grinned. "I am. And maybe my love story has found its ending after all," he said.

"Huh?"

"The new play I'm working on. The ending hasn't been clear."

Surprised, she tipped her head to see him better. "I thought you had to know the ending before starting the first page."

"You remember me saying that?"

"I-I remember too many things…." His quick smile, the lick of hair he brushed from his forehead, the spicy fragrance of his aftershave…the study sessions at school. And singing together one Christmas in her hometown. Doug had mentioned it weeks ago. That memory had stayed with them both.

He brushed a kiss on her temple. "You sound sad and I'm sorry."

She twisted positions so she could see him. Slowly, she stroked his cheek.

"Doug…I'm happy you're here. Don't doubt it for a moment. But we need to go slowly."

He grinned. "I think it's a little late for 'slow.'"

She waved her hand at the room and down at the bed. "You and I...? We have a history, and this—this is only one part of it. We were happy then, and it's easy to fall into old ways."

"We were simply interrupted, Jen, but I hear you. If you want slow, then okay. What are you doing tomorrow night?"

She laughed. "That's your idea of slow?"

"Weekends don't count."

"Oh, Doug. It's all so familiar, and yet so new. I need to get to know you again."

"I haven't changed. Still ambitious, still love what I do. And still..."

She read the unspoken thought in his eyes. Eyes that shone with love for her. She squeezed his hand.

"The thing is...I need to know not only you, but myself a little better, too. How can I give my heart if I don't know what's in it?"

She heard him draw in a deep breath and let it out slowly. "Maybe," he began, "you've been spending too much time taking care of everyone else and forgotten about yourself."

A week ago, she would have protested. She would have argued loudly. Tonight, she let his words sink in.

CHAPTER SEVEN

A new beginning with Doug. She wanted it and she wanted it to be right this time. But too much introspection always made her nervous. Those diary entries she was forced to make, and that shrink they'd gone to…all good for the others, but none of it did a thing for her. She'd just gone through the motions and coped by keeping herself busy.

Like now. She extended her hand to her first clients of the day, a couple about her parents' age when they'd died, and prepared to assist them, explain options and help them plan for a secure financial future.

Her siblings and she had inherited nothing after the accident. Just a house with a mortgage. Not even a car. Tough when the supermarket was two miles away. Lisa had dropped out of law school and gotten a teaching job as a way to earn a salary, while Jen worked out a budget.

And six months later, Mike and Lisa had married. For all their sakes. God, why was she thinking about this now?

"Let's talk about your goals," she began, "and the type of investments you're comfortable with."

"Not too much risk," said the woman. "Someday one of us will be alone, and we don't want to be dependent on anyone, especially not on our kids."

Jen had been dependent. Sixteen years old and caught in a whirlwind of uncertainty. Her friends couldn't handle it and had stopped coming by. She'd wanted to run away...had a plan to emancipate herself. But Lisa and Mike had stopped that.

"I understand exactly what you mean," said Jen. "Financial planning means security. It's not greed. It's just smart. And I'd never want to be dependent on anyone, either." Never again.

"So you really do understand. Did we give you our children's names as beneficiaries?"

"Yes, you did," said Jen, scanning her computer screen. "As well as their socials. You're good parents."

Her folks hadn't left a will. They'd had a small life insurance policy that didn't go far. Jen winced, annoyed at herself. Her folks had been wonderful in every other way. They'd left a legacy of music and laughter, of warmth and love. She blinked hard and forced her thoughts back to the computer.

By the time her clients left her office, Jen was smiling. She'd done a good job counseling the couple. They seemed much more relaxed than when they'd arrived, confident with their decisions. Just as important, however, she'd returned to being Jen, the consummate professional.

Thinking about the past caused emotional upheavals that wore her out. But what was that old saying? *An unexamined life was not worth living.* She supposed there was some truth to that, but she'd had enough self-examination for a while.

Now she was off to a rehearsal for the community concert coming up next Saturday. With a light heart, she made her way to the Commonwealth Theater, where she might run into Doug.

##

On the night of her concert, Jen looked out at the audience and quickly spotted her "people" in the second row. Every member of her family had come, even Lisa, who'd said she needed an outing in the real world. Baby Brianna and her big brother were safely at home with Mike's doting parents. Her brothers came willingly, knowing they were headed out the next day to Cape Cod for their summer baseball teams and jobs. As for Doug — she peered into the darkening theater toward the back, where he was able to buy one of the few remaining tickets. Someone was waving madly out there. She giggled. Now, she conceded that *all* her people were in attendance.

That notion, as it popped into her head, made her realize that Doug's place in her life had become ever more important. She supposed he was as unforgettable as the song of the same name she'd be singing that night, an unexpected second solo due to illness of the original singer.

She caught the eye of her *Unforgettable* partner backstage. "Are we good to go?"

"I should be asking you that question."

Jen smiled. "I'm all set. The show must go on, right?"

And then there was no more time for chit-chat. Jen made her way to the risers and took her place. Excited for sure. But…happy as well. She stood taller and felt more carefree than she had in a long time.

She focused on the director, joined in the beginning medley of standards and knew the chorus had come through when she heard the initial applause. Duets, trios, and solos followed. She breathed deeply as her cue for "Summertime" drew closer. And then she was in the spotlight.

The familiar melody slid from her diaphragm, and as she continued, she felt herself smile, totally enjoying and losing herself in the words. She riffed on the melody, improvising and feeling free, as though she were the one in the song spreading her wings, flying away. The musicians followed her, and unlike a karaoke number, the music they made together was rare and so personal—so Jen! She reveled in it until the end…when it became too personal. The words weren't true for her. Some things had harmed her. Her dad and mom could not stand by. They were gone when she'd still needed them. Even though she'd sung this lyric many times, tonight, emotion choked her and her voice broke. Her heart broke…again, while tears ran down her cheeks.

Thunder assaulted her ears. Confused, she carefully turned her head to the left, then to the right, and then, second by slow second, returned to reality. The audience was on their feet. Clapping, whistling, and shouting *bravo, bravo.*

Lisa and Emily were crying. She scanned for Doug and spotted him jogging down the aisle right to the stage. In his hand, a small bouquet.

"It was supposed to be for later, but timing is everything. No more tears, Henny-Penny. Take another bow. You're a hit!"

The guy always managed to make her laugh.

##

"You were great, sis. Just great. We're proud of you," said Andy. "It was an *unforgettable* performance!"

"Very pun-ny. But very nice to hear from a younger brother."

"We're glad we came," added Brian. "Timing was close since we're heading out tomorrow." His grin said it all, and Jen knew his mind was already on the pitcher's mound.

"Thanks, boys. I've enjoyed my fifteen minutes of fame, but now reality awaits."

She walked hand in hand with Doug outside the theater as their group looked for Luis and the car. "Actually, guys, I think I'm supposed to drive you to Hyannis tomorrow for your summer league. With all the rehearsals and night classes, I'm a bit confused. But I'm ready to go."

"You can sleep late," said Brian. "Mike bought us a car."

"He what?" Jen exclaimed.

"It's an almost-new second-hand Pilot," said Andy, "so there's room for our stuff." He patted her arm. "The gas is on us."

Totally baffled, Jen turned to her brother-in-law. "I could have driven them...why did—" Mike had done so much for them already. Regardless of his income, enough was enough.

"Both you and Lisa have busy lives. Neither of you can go and fetch them every time they want to come home."

"But I would have..." she began to protest.

"He's right, Jen." Doug's quiet voice caught her attention. "Your brothers are old enough to be responsible for a car. With the baseball scholarships they just told me about, and the attention they'll get from the scouts, who knows where they'll end up? They'll need a car anyway."

71

She took a breath before saying, "I know where they'll end up. They're staying right here in Boston. They'll play for the Red Sox!"

The boys cheered. Lisa laughed. Doug said, "Hear, hear!" The tension was cut.

"But that's not the way it works," said Mike, the only one who'd been through a professional draft experience. "And there's no use speculating. The only rule in this family is that our kids graduate first. And that's not debatable."

"Definitely," said Jen quickly. "Can't take a chance on being sidelined with a broken arm or something worse." Like never getting drafted by any team. Without her degree, she'd be nowhere. Their hardworking parents had pushed education, had wanted a better life for their kids. And then Mike, the boys' legal guardian, had picked up where her folks had left off. He was determined her brothers understand the importance of backup plans.

"Besides," said Mike, throwing his arm around Andy, "they're not ready to go pro. They need a little more meat on their bones. Eat, boys, eat!"

Jen glanced at Doug. "You were skinny at their age, too."

"Live in the present, Henny-Penny. Can't call me skinny now."

He had her there. "Not going to argue. I guess time has a way of changing things." She looked at the ones she loved, her personal crowd—and the truth of her statement slammed into her like a runaway train.

"My God," she said, suddenly shivering. "Our lives really are changing. I don't like it!" She took a deep breath, her gaze slowly moving from one beloved person to the other. "I can't stop any of you from growing up and branching out, but one thing must not change. We will always be the Delaneys! The Delaney-Brennan clan.

We stick together no matter what, because if we don't, we might disappear like…like"—she waved her fingers—"ashes in the wind."

"Promise me." she added, her voice cracking. Her chin dropped.

Silence followed, broken in a moment by a cacophony of voices. Familiar, reassuring voices. Mike's protective tone, her brothers' tentative expressions, Lisa's sympathetic hugs. But only one voice registered.

"Let it go, Jen. Let the damn fear go!" Doug leaned in, his forehead touching hers. "Your family's not going anywhere, and they don't need a babysitter. Not anymore. Now, it's your turn. Do what the song said and spread your wings. It's time."

Maybe Doug was right, in theory. Not in reality. Not a babysitter, but a coach?

A week later, Jen sat behind the wheel of Mike's car, heading west on the Mass Pike toward the Tanglewood Music Center in Lennox. She darted a glance at Doug, who sat next to her.

"Emily's awfully quiet back there," she whispered. "Will you take a look? A subtle look. She's sensitive."

"Sure," said Doug, twisting in his seat. "Hey, Emily. What's going on in that head of yours?"

"Geez. I said subtle!" said Jen.

"You can probably tell what's going on," said Emily. "I'm an open book. Everybody can read me. I wish…I wish I was stronger, like you, Jen."

"Oh, Emmy. I've got my own issues…as Doug likes to remind me. But you? You're terrific. Just consider how you're spending this summer! You've earned a fantastic opportunity."

"You mean by my audition?"

"And the recommendations from your teachers, and getting all the paperwork in on time."

"…and convincing Mike to let me out of his sight for the summer with no adult supervision. I guess I'm an adult"

"Yeah, a bit overprotective is our big brother."

"He always says if my head weren't attached to my shoulders, I'd forget where I put it. And he may be right. Like..uh…right now. Jen, I forgot my money!"

"What?" Typical. Which was why Jen was still Lisa's deputy.

"I forgot the credit gift card Mike gave me to use at Tanglewood. It's on my desk at home. It was for lunches and other 'incidentals' that aren't included in the program. He said the safest thing to do is use a gift card. I think it was for five hundred dollars."

Great. She had only twenty dollars in her wallet. Her mind raced for solutions, but Doug's laughter interrupted her thoughts. She glared. "What's so funny? Do you want her to starve?"

"Just watching you think," he replied with a grin. "You're very expressive when problem-solving." He turned to look at Emily. "Not to worry, honey. Your sister has a knack for rescuing people."

"Oh, come on. This one's actually a no-brainer. Even you could figure it out." She waved her fingers at her sister. "We'll just stop at an ATM, and I'll withdraw enough from my account to keep you going for a week. There's no way, however, that I'm giving you five hundred in cash."

Emily sighed a big sigh. "I don't blame you. I'd probably lose it."

"Amazing how you never lose your violin," said Doug, a meaningful note in his voice.

"Doug! I'd never, ever do that." Emily's indignation now had both Doug and Jen laughing.

"I believe you. Just teasing," said Doug.

"But…you know…money will be an issue real soon. Do I have any money of my own, Jenny? You know, like from Mom and Dad?"

If only. "I'm sorry, sweetie. I thought you already knew that from when we discussed it with the boys."

"So Lisa and Mike pay for everything?"

"They sure do. Before I started my career, I had some scholarship money, and I worked part-time in school," said Jen. "But Lisa and Mike provided our home and food and clothing. So why are you asking all these questions now?"

"It's a violin thing. I'll figure it out."

Jen's mind filled with possibilities. "Do not ask Mike to fund a Stradivarius or any other rare instrument. Hear me, Emily? Do not. Enough is enough! And that's way beyond a normal expense."

"I might not be-be worthy of one anyway."

"Do you want to be?" asked Doug.

"More than anything."

"Then you'll get there. First, however, make the most of the summer. You'll be with true professionals, and they'll have some good advice."

"I can't wait to see Maestro Perlman again," said Emily, addressing Doug directly. "He really wanted me to go to Julliard in New York, where he teaches master classes," she told him, shaking her head. "But I was too scared to leave Boston."

Silence resonated for a moment. "Sounds awfully familiar…" The deep voice next to Jen offered thoughtfully. "Staying home seems to run in your family."

"You had lots of options, Em," said Jen. "But The New England Conservatory is a fabulous school, too. You're not being cheated."

"The Maestro said the same thing when I told him at music camp last summer. He understands me, and he said when I was ready to fly, I should let him know."

"I have a feeling," said Doug slowly, "that when the time comes, your violin issue will take care of itself."

"Doug's probably right. And I'm beginning to feel like the most ordinary person in this car!"

The bit of levity lightened the mood, but Jen continued to think about her sister's dream. The "violin issue" wouldn't take care of itself. Nothing ever resolved itself, except a common cold. She had to come up with a future plan.

##

"Your sister is going to have a fabulous summer," said Doug as he and Jen headed back to the car after waving goodbye to Emily.

"I think so, too. At least she can't complain about the campus. Hundreds of acres surrounded by scenery an artist would paint. I just hope it's everything she dreamed it would be."

"Dreams take a lot of work. And sometimes, as the song tells us, we get what we need instead of what we want."

"I suppose. But none of us are willing to settle…at least not yet. And that includes you!" Jen took out the car keys and offered them to Doug. "Feel like driving? Suddenly, I'm wiped."

He took the keys and kissed her. "Sometimes being a big sister is hard work. I don't think I gave Eve an ounce of concern compared to how you guys act. Guess I wasn't a great big brother."

"Don't beat yourself up. From what you've told me, you were trying to cope with some family dynamics yourself."

"You may have a point," he said, kissing her again. This time she blushed, and his heart filled. "Let's go. Maybe, just maybe, it's time to reevaluate."

With her hand on the door, she tilted her head back to see him. "What do you mean?"

"Want to take a little detour to chez Collins?"

Her eyes widened, a grin started. "Wouldn't miss it for the world."

They headed east and left the Mass Pike at the next exit. Doug had no expectations, but felt his stomach tighten. Despite his protestations to the contrary, was it possible he still sought approval from the people who should have been his natural cheerleaders? He'd thought he was beyond caring about his folks' opinions.

"They might not even be home," he muttered.

Jen massaged his shoulder. Sweet. "It'll be fine," she said. "Either they'll confirm your beliefs, or you'll have a happy surprise. Regardless, you won't have to wonder anymore."

True. "I love your analysis," he said, "realistic with a hint of optimism. And I hope you still feel that way if this is a total bust."

And there was the crux. He wanted Jen to know the good, the bad and the ugly. He'd been honest in all other ways—school, career, relocation—but somehow, his family had remained hidden. He reached for her hand, and she tucked it into his.

"This time around," he began, "I want everything in the open. Maybe you've never given my family a second thought. But I'm in deep with you, Jen, and now I want no secrets."

She pulled her hand away. "I hear you, believe you, but Doug…I'm not quite ready. You're moving too fast."

His breath caught; his thoughts spun. Jen's mind continued to rule her heart. Fear still nipped at her, and

she clung to a safety zone. In total contradiction to when
he held her in his arms. In her bed, she'd received him
lovingly, with heart and soul. He breathed again.

"Take all the time you want, Henny-Penny. I'm not
going anywhere."

##

Doug drove down one of the town's main streets, turned
right for several blocks and approached the
neighborhood of one-story, wood-sided homes where he
grew up. He gazed at the familiar setting. As usual, some
front lawns were well-tended, uniformly green and
trimmed; others needed weeding. And yet other homes
needed a paint job.

"It all seems both familiar and strange," he said. "I
know every street, but basically, I feel like an outsider,
evaluating the area like a Realtor would. And yet, I lived
here for eighteen years. A long time."

He felt Jen's hand on his thigh.

"I feel the same way about Woodhaven. It's—it's a
place I used to know. Mike's parents still live across the
street from my old house." Her voice faded. He pressed
her hand to his mouth and kissed it.

"I wouldn't imagine you enjoy visiting there."

"I don't, but I also don't like to disappoint Aunt
Irene and Uncle Bill," she said, "the senior Brennans.
Fortunately, we celebrate most holidays in Boston.
Mike's brother lives in town, too."

"Good. That'll make it easier going forward." He
pulled to the curb a block from his parents' home and
reached for his cell phone.

"A surprise might not go over well," he said as he
connected. Then, "Hey, Dad...Yeah, it's Doug. I'm in
the area and thought I'd stop by..."

"...Okay, ten minutes. See ya then."

He put the phone down. "My mom's in the shower. They're meeting friends for dinner, so this will be a quick visit. Better that way."

"Fair enough," said Jen. "They have a life, too. And besides, I'm kind of hungry myself. Lunch seems like ages ago."

On cue, her stomach rumbled. They eyed each other and burst into laughter that seemed to last forever.

"Now I know why it's called 'the best medicine,'" said Doug. "You can meet the parental units and then we'll have a nice dinner. Together. Alone. Don't even think of joining them."

"I actually hadn't, but now that you mention it…"

But her eyes twinkled and her grin teased. He moved toward her and cupped her face with his hands. "Come here," he whispered, before he leaned closer and captured her mouth with his.

Her response was everything he could wish for. "Ah, Jenny, Jenny…"

She slowly pulled back, her breaths audible. "Ah, Dou-gie, Dougie, you'd better drive."

"Yes, ma'am," he replied. And though in this familiar setting, he had to admit that the old insecurities and disappointments had momentarily reared up again, suddenly, it didn't matter at all anymore what his parents thought or did or said about him.

##

"Well, she's a pretty one!" said Doug's father as he opened the door. "Maybe there's hope for you yet."

Jen felt her smile fade.

"Dad!"

"Eddie!" came a woman's voice.

"What? What did I say?"

Clueless. The big man looked truly confused, and Jen didn't know whether to laugh or cry.

"For goodness sakes, Ed. Where are your manners?" A tall, trim woman with curly dark hair came forward and offered her hand. "I'm Doug's mom, Helen. It's nice to meet you."

"Likewise," said Jen.

The woman turned to her son. "You doing okay?" she asked, giving him a hug.

"Sure."

"Good." She patted his shoulder and led them into the living room. Jen sat on one end of the upholstered sofa with Doug next to her. A few prints hung on the walls. "Doug hasn't brought any friends by since...I don't know, maybe since high school."

"I haven't lived here since high school!" said Doug.

"That's true enough," said his mom, a quick smile flashing across her face as she sat on a club chair. "But just in case...I keep your old room clean and ready. Eve's too."

Doug's mouth opened and closed, but no sound came forth. He looked stunned.

Jen poked at him. "At a loss for words, playwright?"

"I never know what to expect," he muttered. Finally, he stopped staring at his mom. "You can finally turn the room into that craft room you always wanted. Or a library. Or a home office. Mom...I'm okay. I'm fine. So, redecorate to your heart's content."

Helen glanced at Doug's father.

"You earning a living?" asked the man, finally sitting down near his wife. "Tell me you're earning a decent paycheck like your friends here do, and your mother will redecorate. Their folks are always bragging. I know more about their kids than about my own son."

Doug's folks are nothing like mine were. Where's the warmth? The atmosphere is such a downer!

His dad still commanded attention. "Georgie's working for the gas company, like his dad and me. Making a steady paycheck. And Tommy Belson joined the air force, and that wasn't an easy thing. He's climbing the ranks. And who was that little guy, the one who skied like the wind? Well, he's part of the Mt. Snow operation—assistant director or something big. All good boys."

"You're talking about Peter Davis," said Doug. "The best skier on the mountain. Glad to hear he's doing something he loves."

"And making a living," said Eddie. He glanced at Jen, then back at Doug. "Parents think about these things. Your mother worries about you." He turned to Helen. "And don't deny it."

The woman bit her lip. "Anyone care for some iced tea? Lemonade? I've got both in the fridge." She stood and faced the kitchen.

"We don't want to detain you," said Jen, starting to rise. "Doug said you've got a dinner date with friends."

Helen glanced at her watch. "We can postpone for ten minutes. I want to visit with my son."

Point for Helen.

Jen sat back down.

"Evie told us you'd bunked in with her," said Doug's father.

"For a few days, until I found my own place."

Ed turned to Jen. "My daughter's an intern at Mass General. Dr. Eve Collins. Won't have to think twice about her."

Jen nodded. "I suppose not."

"She's happy, Dad. Working hard but loving it."

The man's grin lit his face.

"Which is what everyone strives for," added Jen. "Why work forty hours or more a week at something you hate? Doesn't make sense to me."

"You sound like another dreamer," said Ed, looking from Jen to Doug. "What a pair, thinking money grows on trees."

She sensed Doug about to rise and tugged him back. Jen leaned toward his father. "Have you ever seen Doug's plays?"

He looked blank for a moment. "Oh, in school. I think we drove across one time." He looked at his wife. "Right?"

"The play made me cry."

"And that's when I said, no more," said Ed. "Who wants to see a play that makes my wife cry?"

Jen stood and stared at Doug's father. "I know the answer to that one," she said. "Thousands of people do. Every week, several thousand people buy tickets to see *The Broken Circle* on Broadway. How can you not know that?"

"They know," said Doug joining her. "I sent them tickets for opening night last year, but they didn't come."

"Your mother had a cold and a-a fever," Eddie protested. "Besides, it's expensive to stay at a hotel in New York and too far to drive back at night…

"I did see the play," interrupted Helen quietly.

Her husband swiveled toward her, and she continued. "I took the early bus to Port Authority, went to a matinee, and took the bus back home." She strolled over to place a hand on Doug's arm. "I cried even harder, but I loved it."

Silence descended until Doug said, "You're the heroine in this drama, Mom, that's for sure." Then he put his arm around her shoulder and kissed her cheek.

Jen glanced at Doug's father. The man looked flummoxed. "I think it's time we made an exit," she said to Doug before addressing Helen. "Glad to meet you, Mrs. Collins. I'm also glad you like the theater."

"Oh, are you a writer like Doug?" asked Helen.

Jen chuckled. "Sorry. In fact, you might say that writing is my least favorite thing."

"Really? How curious."

Doug's dad left his chair and stepped closer. "So, what do you do for a living? Maybe something practical?"

Jen winked at Doug, then faced his dad. "You could say I help people. I really help them a lot, teaching them how to budget. Oh, and I also sing."

Eddie moved aside. "Figures. Between the two of them, Helen, they probably earn zilch. Nothing. nothing steady. She sounds like a social worker."

"I didn't say that, Mr. Collins," Jen protested. "Life is complicated, and people are looking for all kinds of advice these days. I happen to be good with numbers." She told no lies, but when she imagined how little support the man had given Doug throughout the years, she chose not to enlighten him further.

He nodded and reached into his back pocket. "Do you need any money, son?"

LINDA BARRETT

CHAPTER EIGHT

Back in the car, Jen's thoughts remained on Doug's father. "Family dynamics can be tricky," she said, "not so much black-and-white as shades of gray.

"Were there 'shades of gray' in your house?" he challenged.

Her thoughts flew backward. She'd been lucky to have parents who made a fuss about a kindergarten picture, cheered at a baseball game or for a test score—always encouraging, always praising. And sometimes making suggestions.

"Maybe we were too young..." she began.

"You were not too young," countered Doug. "Neither was Lisa. Teenage years could wreak havoc in a family."

Jen paused, thinking back carefully. "I wreaked havoc, as you say, only after they were gone. I gave Lisa and Mike a few big headaches."

"Understandable."

"Ancient history." She patted his thigh. "I'm glad you were able to turn down your dad's offer. I suspect he's not as bad as he seems."

"Maybe, maybe not. That was guilt talking. He was trying to make Mom happy. I-I can't quite process that she snuck down to the city to see the show and never told anyone. Not even me!"

"That's what mothers do. For their children, anything. As for Eddie, well he knows about her trip now."

"It shook him up. Therefore, he offered his son, the playwright, money, which he thinks will calm the water."

But Jen wasn't sure that was the only reason. "Maybe he loves his son. Maybe he worries about you."

"Ha!"

"One thing's for sure," said Jen. "He may be awkward and blustery, but he loves your mom."

"If he'd exchange the bluster for a little bit of tenderness, sometimes, and maybe tell her out loud how he feels…she'd be better off."

Jen shrugged. "That's her lecture to give, and if she ever gets to a breaking point, she will."

"Which leads to her turning point."

"What?"

"'All the world's a stage…'" quoted Doug. "We all play out our dramas. My parents are no different, living in their one-story ranch house in western Massachusetts. Drama lives in every house on their street, in every home in the world. Joy, despair, grief and hope…there always has to be hope…and then decisions are made. A path is chosen or a new idea brings an aha moment and changes a person inside."

With those words, Jen glimpsed a window into Doug's soul. "My God. That's how you write your plays! You see these things. You capture these events, these emotions. And you can make others feel them."

Silence was his only answer for a moment.

"Yeah, I guess I do," he finally replied. "But I'm not only an observer. I've lived through the highs and lows myself. Here's how I look at it: everyone searches for a peaceful, vanilla life, but in the end, they find that life is mint chocolate chip, and rocky road. Vanilla is an unreliable goal."

"Oh-h-h...." Jen clutched her stomach at her aha moment. "You're right," she whispered. "Vanilla is the safer road. I've planned for it, fought for it. But then something happens, and—and..."

"You're hijacked. Staring at new choices on a rocky road."

Although their conversation lingered, Jen was on familiar turf the next morning and could fall into her comfortable role. The only choices she'd be making were financial ones with her clients. She unlocked her computer and began scrolling, but stopped at the company-wide announcement of Matthew's promotion and move to Kentucky. His last day at headquarters was the upcoming Friday.

Her heart sank for a moment, but she tried to rally. No vanilla here. She'd consider it a pistachio event—for them all. Hopefully a wonderful turning point for Matt. But what if the offer had been hers? What if she'd turned it down because she wanted the safer road? What if that safer choice ultimately destroyed her career?

She refocused on the screen. Ridiculous thoughts. If she kept it up, she'd soon be competing with Doug in the drama department.

##

Workwise, Doug shouldn't have taken time off to go with Jen to Tanglewood. On Monday night, he was buried in scripts. Revisions to *The Sanctuary* came first. Amazing how actors, by bringing the story to life, and by reacting to the writing, could clearly show him where adjustments were needed, where he could fix a phrase that may have seemed good on paper, but when spoken…not so much. He grabbed the chance to revise and make changes for the better.

He glanced at the clock. After ten. Shoot, he was late with his call. That ten o'clock connection had become a nice habit. He reached for his cell, but it rang before he could connect. Jen.

Smiling, he answered it. "Hi sweetie. I lost track of time."

"I figured. You must be elbow-deep in breaking points and turning points and drama."

"Hey, you really listened!"

"Oh, yeah. And another turning point is coming up. Matt's last day is Friday. Liz's, too. Feel like joining the gang for our private farewell party?"

As if he'd miss it. "Maguires?"

"The scene of many crimes."

"I'll be there, but not sure exactly when."

"Crunch time?"

"Something like that."

"You wasted the day with me yesterday. You should've been working."

"Listen up, sweetheart. No time spent with you is wasted. Remember that. I'm used to pulling all-nighters."

Her laugh was as light as a moonbeam. "Like we were still in school. I remember us cramming for exams, testing each other…

"Keep remembering the good stuff, Jenny. I've still got deadlines, projects, and a new curriculum for the fall to finalize. It's all good. And being here, with you again...what can I say? It's everything."

"I-I...

"Shush. No pressure. I'm a patient man." He hadn't known just how patient until now. He'd give her all the time she needed to find the real Jen, the girl she'd turned her back on years ago.

"I'll say only one thing," Jen began slowly.

Her tone of voice put him on alert. "And what would that be?"

"I-I'm glad you came back. Our ending was...rough. But we're adults now. Whatever happens between us this time won't be so emotional."

He tried not to laugh. Where did she get her ideas? "Is that right, my Henny-Penny? Are you saying that love is totally rational? Logical?"

"Oh, don't put words in my mouth. I didn't say anything at all about love. It's just-just... oh, forget it."

But he wouldn't forget her confusion, her effort to avoid sharing that deepest of all emotions. "You do realize you'd put every songwriter out of business if love were a purely rational thing. But still, you're giving this man some hope. I think my next play will be called, *The Courtship of Jennifer Delaney.* It will be an opus, running 568 pages and taking ten hours to present."

"You'll lose a bundle on that one!" she said, amusement in her voice. "Not worth it."

"Let me decide about that. Sweet dreams, Jenny." He almost danced around his apartment after disconnecting. Pushing *The Sanctuary* aside, he pulled over *Straight from the Heart.* There was no one like Jennifer Delaney for a bit of inspiration. If Steve Kantor wanted to see a play instead of a novel, he'd get a play. With renewed energy, he began to read. Soon his fingers tapped the keyboard, and by three o'clock in the morning, he'd shaped the first act.

No matter how long it took his logic-only love to listen to her heart, he'd be waiting.

At her crowded table in Maguire's, Jen glanced at her watch for the third time and then looked toward the door—again. If Doug didn't show up pretty darn quick, he'd starve. Tonight's send-off for Matt and Liz had morphed into a party of friends who'd taken up three tables and had already scoffed down platters of wings and meatballs, not to mention beer. And now the wait staff was taking dinner orders.

"Oh, well…" she murmured, "his loss."

"Talking to yourself?" asked Alexis, "Or to the guy who just walked through the door?"

Jen swiveled around, spotted Doug, and felt her tension ease. "It's just that he said he'd be here," she protested, "said he wouldn't miss it…"

Alexis laughed and patted her arm. "Man, you've got it bad. Doug seems like a great guy. I hope it works out for you."

"Thanks," said Jen, watching Doug weave his way through the tables. "But I'm not sure…"

"Typical," Alexis replied with a dismissive wave. "You should have seen my sister after meeting John, who is now her husband. What a wreck she was. almost-walking-into-walls kind of wreck. She was up, down and sideways. But I've never seen her happier than now."

"Really? Lisa and Mike were different," Jen said, ruminating. "Crazy about each other from Day One. It was only later…because of us…"

Alexis squeezed her hand. "Forget it. Live in the present. And speaking of presents…here's yours. Hi, Doug."

"Sorry I'm late," he said, after greeting the crowd in general. He slipped into the booth across from Jen, leaned over and kissed her quickly on the mouth.

She responded as naturally as if they touched every day. *Oh, God, this is too easy. What am I doing? Is it just a habit? How will I know? Stop! Stop thinking. There's no rush.*

"What a week," continued Doug, smiling at her, "and the weekend looks almost the same...except...for this." He whipped out a pair of tickets. "A gift from the theater management. Red Sox game tomorrow night at 7:05. Wanna go?"

"Of course, she does," said Alexis.

"I'm right here, girlfriend." Jen rolled her eyes at Alexis before turning her attention to Doug. "I'd rather watch my brothers play in their summer league, but since that's out, I'll settle for Fenway and the Red Sox."

"Knowing your family, maybe one day, your brothers really will play at Fenway Park." Doug grabbed a lonely fry and popped it into his mouth. "Cold, but I'm hungry. Worked through lunch. No finger foods for me tonight."

"You're too late anyway," said Jen, "but now you're in luck. Bonnie's here to take your order. Maybe she'll feel sorry for you and rush it."

She listened to him chat up their usual server, creating an instant rapport, and was amazed at the amount of food he wanted.

He glanced at her when he was finally done. "What? What?"

"Is my expression so readable?" Jen asked with a laugh. "You've ordered enough for five people."

"Tomorrow's lunch is in there. I won't have to waste time making something."

He looked so pleased with himself, she wanted laugh. But she also wanted to know more. "So, are you drowning or just totally immersed?"

"Totally immersed and feeling great. But always thinking about the deadline. This baby opens in three short months. September 14th, to be exact. Mark it in your calendar!"

She'd engrave it in her memory. "Looks like no summer vacation for you, that's for sure."

"There's always next year. This play's more important now."

"I understand that," she said, nodding, but then teased, "so you won't be jealous when I'm at the Cape? I usually take long weekends, which seem so short! In fact, the whole summer always seems to speed by every year. I guess I like the beach!"

"Time's a funny thing, Jenny. It's elastic. It speeds by when you're happy and busy, and crawls when you're miserable. When I first got to New York— hmm….someday, I'll tell you how slow motion feels."

Their lighthearted conversation darkened. She'd thought he'd forget about her with all the new challenges he'd faced in the Big Apple. She'd told herself what they'd had was a puppy love. But the longing in his gaze at that moment put a lie to that.

"Wow," she whispered ruefully. "I knew it would be tough. but my idea wasn't meant to…."

His smile returned as though it had never disappeared. "Right now, I have an idea you're going to love." He stood and called out to the couple of honor, urging Matt and Liz to the table.

"How about you guys plan on a trip back here for opening night of *The Sanctuary*. It'll give all of us something extra to look forward to —an excuse for a big reunion."

Jen watched her girlfriend's smile grow while Matt nodded. "If we can swing it, we sure will."

"Oh, we'll swing it," said Liz. "I'm excited about Kentucky, but I'm determined not to lose touch with my friends here. My mom still has friends from her childhood, and that is one attribute I want to emulate."

"Oh, Liz, I'm so glad," said Jen. Impulsively, she squeezed her friend's hand. "We've got to find time."

"No, Jennifer. We've got to *make* time. Laziness is out! My mother said it takes effort. 'Don't stand on ceremony. Pick up the phone,'" she always told me.

"She's never heard of email?" asked Matt. "Texting's even better."

"She had plenty to say about that, too! Nothing replaces a phone call or a real visit. So your idea is perfect, Doug. We'll be here."

Jen watched the couple walk away and chat with others. Tears stung her eyes, which surprised her.

"Jenny! What's wrong?"

She shook her head. "Nothing. Nothing. I'm just an idiot." And now he'd have questions. The guy was totally tuned into her.

"You won't lose Lizzy, sweetheart. You heard her."

"I know. It's just..." Well maybe he deserved the truth. "I'm not Liz." She could barely get the words out.

"And?" he replied softly, his tone neutral.

She glanced up. "Tuned in" was barely the right expression. He was laser- focused on her. "I admire her attitude. She's brave to go so far away. Despite everything, I-I still don't think I could do it," she whispered, as tears threatened once more. And if she couldn't, she'd disappoint him again.

In an instant, he stood next to her. "C'mon." He pulled her up and held her close. "No one's forcing you, Jen. I'm certainly not. And think about this: if that confession is upsetting you… you've actually opened yourself to possibilities."

Had she? For a long time, the idea of leaving her family had been a closed door. She'd slammed it shut and thrown away the key. Until Doug had come back. Until she'd opened up her eyes to those around her, like Liz and Matt. She'd hidden her head when other co-workers had relocated, but she couldn't hide this time. Liz was a real friend. So was the rest of her Friday night crew. "I guess nothing stays the same," she admitted, "and that gives me a stomachache."

"I know."

"Are you a shrink in disguise?" she asked, suddenly suspicious, and suddenly recalling that he'd minored in psychology. "Sometimes I think you know me better than I know myself."

He cocked his head, and a tiny smile emerged. But all he said was, "Don't give me too much credit, Jenny. You're not as unique as you might imagine. Everyone gets uptight when changes hit them."

"And then?"

He nodded at the couple approaching the mic. Matt and Liz. "And then, I guess, you sing."

She'd been singing all her life, all types of music. But it hadn't made her a braver person. In fact, it provided cover, keeping her too busy to think.

The opening notes started, familiar and perfect, from the Beatles—and perfect for the couple facing a new adventure—who sang about getting by with a little help from their friends.

Jen took it all in while swirling in a whirlpool of emotion—sadness, joy, regret, anger, disappointment. Her friends had found what she had lost.

Not lost, she corrected herself. What she had rejected.

She studied the man who'd been the boy she'd loved. The man who still set her heart racing, the man who seemed to have the patience of Job, at least with her. But he was also a man determined to fulfill his goals and ambitions. A man who wasn't afraid of anything, not even of taking another chance on her.

She closed her eyes, wishing she felt stronger, wishing she could talk to her mom. Lucky Liz.

"If my mom were still here, we wouldn't be in this situation. If my folks were still around…"

"We might not have met," interrupted Doug. "Stop torturing yourself and move on."

She stared at him, wide-eyed. "That sounded fierce."

"It's time, Jen. It's time."

If he only knew how much she agreed, how much she wanted to put the past high on that shelf he'd once mentioned. If he only knew how many doubts she had about herself.

But maybe he did. His warm smile reappeared and reassured. "It'll be all right, Jenny." He turned toward the stage. "Hey, listen up, *Here Comes the Sun!* Perfect."

LINDA BARRETT

CHAPTER NINE

The next morning, Jen hummed the Beatles' tunes from the party, then changed to *Take Me Out to the Ballgame* as she flew through her usual weekend chores. No stranger to household tasks, she was finished by noon and looking forward to enjoying her night out with Doug.

Baseball parks were happy places. So were football stadiums. As soon as someone entered a sports arena, all real-life problems were left outside the gate and forgotten for a while. Tonight would be a delightful interlude where she and Doug could just have fun with the rest of the crowd.

She brought her manicure supplies to the kitchen table just as the phone rang. Without checking the readout, she answered, "Doug?"

"Sorry."

"Lisa! Hello, hello. I'm amazed you found five minutes to call. Has Brianna finally stopped the crying jags and is she letting you get some sleep?"

Silence. "I-I'm afraid not. The pediatrician said she's colicky. She just cries and cries and never sleeps. I massage her, rub her tummy, walk her, hold her and...and I'm so tired, I could cry myself."

"Oh, Lis. I knew you had your hands full, but I didn't know the baby was such a challenge. What does the doctor suggest?"

"Not much. She'll outgrow it by four months."

"Oh." Three months more of non-stop crying. She could think of nothing to counter with. "Where's Mike?"

"He took Bobby outside to play. We wanted to go to the Cape for a couple of weeks before the season starts, but I don't have the desire or the energy."

To her dismay, Jen heard her sister start to cry. Mostly about how tired she was and that she needed to get some sleep.

"I have an idea, Lis, and don't react immediately. How about calling in a baby nurse for a few weeks, just so you can get back to yourself?"

"Now you sound like Mike! But Brianna's *my* baby! I don't want some stranger taking care of her. Mom never had a nurse for you or any of us, not even the twins."

Jen stopped breathing for a moment. Her big, strong sister wasn't immune to allowing the past ruin the present either. It felt too familiar. "Now you listen to me, Lisa Delaney-Brennan. Mom didn't need help. None of us were colicky! We would have heard stories about it if we were. You are a wonderful mother, and you have to do what's right for you and your precious family. And our mother would be the first to tell you the same thing. If it means getting a baby nurse for a couple of weeks or months, then do it! Mike loves you to pieces. He wants you healthy. Heck, we all want you healthy and happy."

She ran out of steam but wanted to cry. Lisa had been the strong one, taking on responsibility no young woman should have had to face. Four younger siblings to raise—with Mike—but those days were tough.

"Jen?" Her sister's voice sounded stronger now.

"Yeah?" Jen replied with caution. Was Lisa going to argue?

"Was this what you meant about the Delaney-Brennan clan supporting each other?" Somehow, laughter filled Lisa's voice now. Jen didn't want to question it.

"It certainly is. Sticking together by being truthful. We're not only sisters, Lis, but we're also friends. That's the way I see it. I love you, and I trust you, and you can count on me, too. I'll come over to babysit whenever you need me. We have each other's backs. Mom and Dad would second my advice. Hire a nurse! And don't feel guilty about it."

Lisa's voice came softly. "When did you get so smart?"

"I'm not smart, Lis, but I-I've been thinking about things lately. I'm trying to process Liz and Matt moving away…and I'm working on other stuff."

"I'm betting Doug Collins figures into all these new ideas you're having."

Her sister was sharp. "Could be."

"Then all I'll say is that he can't take his eyes off you. Maybe this time around will be the right time."

Maybe. "Do you want me to watch Brianna for a few hours so you can get some sleep? It's now or tomorrow. Doug and I are going to Fenway tonight." She couldn't disappoint Doug. She had to show him she could balance family and their time together.

"Enjoy yourself, and thanks for the offer, but I've got it. Maybe I just needed some sister time. Some sister approval. You and I, Jenny, are the ones who share that memory bank of the early years with Mom and Dad. After Mike, you know you're my go-to person."

"And I hope I never let you down," Jen replied. "Sometimes, I still feel I'm your lieutenant, handling the younger ones. But I'm not as concerned today as I was back then. Mike turned out to be one of the good guys."

"I've always known that," said Lisa, "and I thank God for him every day. But Mike's not the last of the good guys. You might have found one yourself."

"You may be right. How about I let you know as soon as I'm sure." She disconnected, realizing she'd misled her sister a little. Doug was definitely one of the good guys. Just thinking about him made her smile. But he deserved a totally devoted partner.

Funny how her siblings thought she was so strong. She'd really been her sister's right hand in the old days, and she'd always come through. But when it came to charting her own path, well…she didn't feel that resilient.

She ambled over to the wall of family pictures in her living room, examining them one by one. The handsome twins with their sparkling green eyes towered over her six months ago! Emily's smile blazed from the frame, a beautiful young adult. Lisa glowed with early pregnancy, her gaze on Mike's beaming face while he held their son. Andy, Brian and Em were maturing into the people they would become. Lisa and Mike had a handle on everything. The younger ones didn't need Jen to solve their little problems anymore.

She stroked the portrait of her parents, which hung center stage in her family gallery. "Your children are growing up, my loves, and you are not here to see it happen, which is just too terrible to dwell on." A kaleidoscope of images came to her mind: little Bobby, named for his grandpa, Emily playing her violin, Lisa finally receiving her law degree after dropping out of law school twice, Andy and Brian on a baseball field—it really was too much—her parents missing all of that.

Thank you both for getting us off to a good start. I know money was always tight—I remember you celebrating every mortgage payment—but you gave us more security that you can imagine. Singing while doing the supper dishes, Dad's corny jokes and his energy. It worked! I still sing, Mom! We all do.

But no song emerged then. Her throat closed, her voice faded and her tears flowed. It didn't matter. She took another breath and collapsed onto the sofa. "Mom...Dad...I need to tell you something important." She inhaled again. "I've met someone. He-he's special. We've had a rough patch, but this guy — Doug Collins — he doesn't give up. More important, I think he understands me. And my fear of letting go. I promise you that we'll always be the Delaney family, but I have a feeling we're all going in different directions. And that scares me. I-I just had to tell you."

She hugged her stomach and let her tears flow. And she could just hear how her dad might advise her.

Everyone is scared, Jennifer. You're not alone. Courage requires a leap of faith, but happiness requires taking that leap with the right partner. Is this Doug the one?

A weight lifted. She sat up straighter and listened harder. Her parents were only a conversation away. Maybe that's why Lisa had filled journals in the beginning. To communicate, to understand. To be more in touch with them...*or with herself.* Yes! That must be it. Maybe that's why Doug wrote plays. He was always trying to make sense of a complicated, messy world. Always trying to find hope in dark places.

Finance was much easier.

She walked closer to the portraits again. If talking to her folks helped her to face her fears, she'd go to them a million times, and never chat with another shrink again. Which she hadn't done in several years.

"I know you're out there somewhere..." she sang softly, as the Moody Blues' lyrics came into her head. Maybe she and Emily had more in common than she'd realized. She'd have to listen more closely the next time her sister played *Amazing Grace.*

##

"It's a wonderful night for a baseball game." Jen paused in their walk toward Fenway Park and pointed upward. "A clear sky, perfect temperature and ..."

"...and we're together," finished Doug, clasping her hand. "Let's get moving, and I'll tell you a story about the oldest ballpark in Major League Baseball."

There wasn't much about Fenway he could tell her that she didn't already know. The Green Monster, The Triangle, The Lone Red Seat. And Neil Diamond's *Sweet Caroline* in the middle of the eighth inning every single game.

"You've got a story for everything," she said, "but I've been here many times—whenever Andy and Brian 'allowed' me to take them!"

Holding hands with Doug felt so right, joking around felt right, too. With her free hand, Jen reached up to brush that stubborn lock of hair from the man's eyes. He snatched her palm and covered it with kisses.

"That makes it official," he said. "We're finally on a real date. No interruptions."

"Yeah. Just you and me...and thousands of others."

This time he stopped walking and pulled her close. "I love you like this, Jen. So relaxed, so joking, so pretty. I knew we could find it again."

She put her finger across his mouth. "No words. Just let the evening play out." But she squeezed his hand and felt herself smile.

They continued strolling to the entrance on Jersey Street. "See how the park blends into the neighborhood. All the buildings are similar," said Doug, gesturing toward the surrounding streets.

"Yes. It's a real city ballpark and a very small one."

"That's for sure. Can't even hold forty thousand fans. So, here's the story: In 1984, Roger Clemens arrived in Boston for the first time and took a taxi to the park." He paused and looked at her. "You do know who Roger Clemens is, don't you?"

Laughing, she nodded. "Pitcher."

"But when the cab arrived, Clemens argued with the driver. Told him Fenway Park was a baseball stadium and this building was nothing but a warehouse!"

"Really?" she asked with a chuckle. "Okay, I hadn't heard that one."

"Want to hear the ending?"

How could she let him down? "Of course, I want the ending."

"The driver told him to look up. And when he did, Clemens saw the stadium light towers and knew he was in the right place."

Just as I am.

"I like it. Wonderful bit of Fenway history." Jen tilted her head back and stared at his familiar face, the face she'd never forgotten, and saw nothing else. Not the park, not the buildings, not the other pedestrians.

"When you smile at me like that…" His voice was raspy as he leaned toward her. She tilted her head back, waiting…and was rewarded. His kiss was strong and exploring. And with his arms snugly around her, Jen's world became rock solid. Until…

"Hey, look at them go!"

"Save it for the KISS-CAM."

"There's a home run in sight, and the game hasn't even started!"

The whistles came, hoots and hollers, too.

"Oh, my God," said Jen, hiding herself against Doug's chest.

His deep laughter was all she heard. "They're just having fun—and they're jealous of the luckiest guy around! But I like the idea of a KISS-CAM. Let the whole world know."

Jen shook her head, basking in her personal discovery. "I'd like to enjoy our own world for a while longer."

"Whatever you want, sweetheart. You call the shots."

They entered the stadium holding hands, until Doug had to produce their tickets. "Hmm…nice. I was too busy working to give it much thought, but we're near center field. We've got to climb, but we'll have a good view."

"Oh, look," said Jen, pointing at the scoreboard. "Red Sox vs. Yankees. What could be better than Boston against New York?" Jennifer grinned up at him. "My brothers would have loved to be here."

"And I'm glad to have you alone!"

They found their seats, not surprised to be surrounded by fans. "Looks like a sold-out game," said Jen.

"You can say that again, girlie," commented the big man sitting next to her with large cup of beer in hand. "And we're gonna show those Yankees how baseball is played in Boston."

"I hope so," she said, before turning toward Doug.

"Want to change seats with me?" Doug asked quietly. "That guy's partying already and the game hasn't even started yet."

Jen patted his hand. "He's just enjoying the anticipation. Do you think a Riders' game with quarterback Mike Brennan is a tea party?"

"Bad analogy, sweetheart. That Boston Tea Party was not a timid event."

"Okay, okay," she said with a groan. "But you get my meaning. And after all, how many Yankee fans would travel here just for a regular game?"

His eyes opened wide. "Are you kidding? A lot. Take a look."

Jen began noting all the navy blue caps with New York's signature white NY in front. Yankee fans were scattered everywhere, including in the row in front of theirs. Doug's observation might have been accurate.

"New York and Boston are really not that far apart," Doug said quietly.

For just a nanosecond, Jen's stomach tightened. But distance was not an issue now. In fact, maybe her tension was an automatic response.

"Point taken. New York is a fine place—to visit."

His laughter was contagious. "From time to time, as needed?"

She nodded.

"Well, that's progress." His quick hug and kiss increased her confidence. Trips to Broadway? She'd handle that.

No score by the end of the third.

"That's what happens when two great teams play each other," said Jen.

"Whatchu talking about, girlie? The Sox rule!" came the voice next to her.

"Not according to the scoreboard yet," answered Jen, pointing at the Green Monster. "Look!"

"Jus' you wait, sister. Jus' you wait."

Jen turned her head toward Doug. "I think our neighbor is taking this game very seriously. And starting to slur his words."

"So is the guy right in front of us — the one with the New York cap. They've been at each other the entire time."

"I know. All I can say is, gedouddahere." Doug laughed. "Exactly right. But now, switch seats with me."

She wrapped her arms around his neck. "You want to be my hero? You want to take those slings and arrows for me?"

Doug stood. "Move over, Ms. Slings and Arrows."

Oh, life was good. She loved this guy. She loved his repartee, his humor, and his intelligence. Had admired those traits years ago and fell hard. Maybe that's why…even when she'd dated others, she'd never given them a real chance.

Cheering and groaning came from the crowd as New York scored a run.

"The Sox aren't ruling now," came the voice from the bleacher below. The guy stood up and glared at the man next to Doug, who wasted no time responding.

"Is that right? You'd better respect where you are. This is Boston!"

"Take it easy, guys," said Doug. "It's only the fourth. Anything can happen. It's still anybody's game."

The New York fan sat back down, and Jen turned to Doug. "I'm spoiled. At the Riders' home games, I'm always in a private box with the family. Now I'm out and about with the real people. Whew!"

"And isn't it fun?" He eye-rolled their neighbors.

New York got another hit and the fan stood up to cheer.

"Sit down, you're blocking the view."

"Whaddayou care? Your team sucks!"

The inning ended, and Boston was now at bat.

And then the magic happened for Beantown. One out. Three men on base, and the next batter hit it hard and high into the stands. Jen figured the noise from the crowd could be heard in the street. The three players on base ran home and Boston had a two-run lead.

Jen's neighbor was quick to strike. "And you said my team sucks? Ha! Can't say that now."

Everything happened fast after that. The NY fan stood, his full cup of beer spilling all over Jen, Doug and the Boston fan, who quickly rose with his fist raised. Doug stepped sideways, shoved both guys away and got punched in the shoulder. "Someone call security!"

"Doug!" Jen cried, trying to pull him back. "Leave them alone. You'll get hurt more." She turned toward new voices. "Oh, good. Security's coming. And they're big."

"We're going quietly, boys," one of the guards said. "This game's over for you."

Jen ignored the rest. "Doug, are you all right?"

"Didn't feel a thing. But look at that. We're famous." He pointed at the big screen where all the action had been covered. "Who needs a KISS-CAM?" He took her in his arms and bestowed the biggest, sweetest, hungriest kiss...and without hesitation, she responded like a thirsty woman stranded in the desert.

"Oh, my love," she whispered. "As long as you're all right."

His hands lingered on her face, fingers gently tracing the contours of her jaw. Blinking twice, he said, "I've never felt better."

"Me, too."

"Ah, Jen. I've dreamed of this."

"You are such a romantic."

His grin warmed her heart. "That I am. And now that I've got you in a tender moment, here's a question: how'd you like to go to New York with me next weekend? I've got to work with the new lead for *The Broken Circle* while she figures out how to 'make the part her own."

CHAPTER TEN

The following Thursday evening, Jen packed a bag for a weekend in New York while still grinning at the reaction to their experience at Fenway. It seemed the whole world had been watching the game that night. Her cell had rung non-stop as Lisa, Mike and her brothers called for details. Liz and Matt called. Alexis offered her opinion that Doug was a "keeper."

"I hear you, I hear you," Jen had replied, "and I'm starting to feel that way myself."

"Good. I think a lot of what happens is about timing. Look at our gang at work. We were all chugging along for a few years, but now things are changing, and sometimes it's hard to adjust. Anyway, I'm glad we're still here in town. At least for now."

Alexis was right about changes, but Jen hummed as she set her bag on the floor. The difference Doug caused in her life now seemed wonderful. Nothing to be afraid of. The knock came exactly as she wheeled the suitcase into the hallway.

"Ready?" asked Doug, examining her face. "You're good with this?"

"A weekend in New York is great. With all that's available for tourists, I can surely keep myself busy while you're working. There's actually a tour of Radio City Music Hall—a behind-the-scenes look. I'd love that."

"Of course, you would! But remember, show time is at eight o'clock. I'd like us both to see the Friday night and Saturday matinee performances."

"Why?" she asked, leading them out the door. "Sounds a bit bor—... ah, too much, no?"

"A bit boring, you say?" But his eyes twinkled. "Not to the playwright. Every audience is different, particularly matinees versus evenings, and I always like eavesdropping and watching reactions to each performance."

"Has the new actress studied the current production?"

"Oh, yeah. She was actually in the original cast in a supporting role for six months. Then went to another show in a bigger role. And when she heard we were going to cast a new lead, she auditioned. She's really good, and I'm sure she'll want to interpret the part her own way."

"Then, I guess you'll have to go back and see her in it?"

"Yup. Her opening is in two weeks."

Something in his voice...a tightness, wariness. "Just think of it as a commute, Jenny. Lots of people do that."

She watched him stow her bag in the trunk of his car and slam the lid.

"I know that. Business is business," she said, "and a playwright always aims for Broadway." Her thoughts raced. They were paying a fortune for a three-night stay at a hotel, and if he had to commute regularly...

"Maybe," she said, hearing her voice quiver, "you shouldn't have given up your apartment. Hotel costs are outrageous."

He spun toward her. "Don't even go there. I couldn't lie to you about that. My home's in Boston now. That's where I want to be."

But maybe not where he should be.

"Besides," he continued. "I can bunk in with Steve Kantor when you're not around. Hopefully, you'll meet him this weekend. He knows the business and we're good friends. Actually, I want to introduce you to everyone, and I'll also take you on a personal tour backstage after the matinee."

Jen absorbed his words and nodded. He was anxious that she understand his world. To make her part of it. Did he simply want to educate her so they could have lively conversations? Or did he want her buy-in so she'd consider making a change in the future? A future that was becoming more definite. In his quiet way, Doug was like a five-star general executing a complex campaign.

##

They stopped off for dinner half-way through the almost five-hour drive, but Doug's mind seemed to be elsewhere. "Just order me anything."

"We're standing in line in a fast food joint," she said. "Hamburger or chicken?"

"I hope you don't mind," he said. "I really don't want to linger over dinner. Next time we'll fly."

She pressed herself against him. "Hey. What's wrong? It's your first time back since you moved. Are you facing a reality check of some kind?"

He snuggled her in close. "The usual. Only twenty-four hours in a day. I'm going to be buried in work the entire weekend." He looked sad, and so apologetic.

"I know that. Business is business behind the scenes. The audience is having all the fun." She reached for their food order and led the way to a table.

"If it will make you feel better, we don't see the starting quarterback of the Boston Riders very much during the season either. He comes, he goes, he sleeps."

His grin slowly emerged. "Then I owe him another one."

"Oh?"

"I once told him I'd hoped to make my own kind of touchdowns one day. And he shook my hand." Doug spoke as he unwrapped his burger. "Eat up."

Jen nodded, but was thinking about her brother-in-law. "Mike's living the American dream himself. Why wouldn't he encourage you?"

Doug's brows rose, his eyes widened. "A career in the arts? C'mon Jen. Most people couldn't imagine it. In fact, they'd discourage it."

But she'd always loved his work. "Forget about your dad. You're proving him wrong."

"But now I see he's got a point. There really is no guarantee every show will be successful." He gathered her hands into his larger one. "I've got to be honest here, Jen." His eyes darkened; his voice was intense. Not knowing what to expect, she took a breath.

"You're scaring me, Doug," she began, her fingers pressing back against his. "You've always been honest with me. So why is today different?"

He cleared his throat. "Today is different," he began slowly, "because for the first time, I'm going to

New York with you. I've always imagined it and now it's real." Leaning forward, he cupped her face with his hands. "Jennifer Delaney, I want you in my life, and I know for that to happen—because of your need for security, your need to feel safe—I must tell you how I make my living."

"You've already told me you were fine. I believed you. Shouldn't I have?" He'd been open with her, so she'd thought.

"I am fine, Jen, stable. And plan to continue that way. But...you never know for sure. The best-laid plans and all that.... And I know that will make you nervous."

She didn't respond, just held her hand up like a cop and thought about his words. "You're right about me," she finally said. "I need some control. But you work hard and have common sense. I don't think you'd let yourself starve."

Then came his laughter, his warm, deep laughter that always stirred her heart. "Only you could come up with that. I love it! Common sense is what most people think creative types *don't* have."

She chuckled with him. "But I know you better than that, Doug. You're not a 'type.' You're unique. At least, to me you are." From laughter to tears. She was on a roller-coaster. "Wh-when you left....it had absolutely nothing to do with money or earning a living or anything like that. And—and as far as I'm concerned, it still doesn't."

And suddenly he was on her side of the booth, cradling her in his arms, kissing her all over her cheeks and mouth and mumbling things about love and royalties.

She started to listen and then to laugh again. His earnest explanations of royalties earned on tickets sold, teaching stints, writing ad copy, editing scripts or even tending bar had her amazed.

"So that's the way it works," he offered. "A playwright does what he needs to do to feed his habit—writing new plays."

"And you do it all," she said. "Well, I know one adjective that could never describe you, Doug."

He looked at her in inquiry. "Rich?"

But she shook her head. "No! Lazy. You're not lazy. You're ambitious. You're talented. And with a little luck...you'll have it all."

She heard him inhale and looked up. "What?"

But he shook his head. "Ready to go?"

##

Their hotel room was half the size of Jen's living room. The closet, the size of a linen closet at home.

"The Big Apple is looking kind of small to me," said Jen, scanning the room in a second. "Actually, pretty tiny."

"It's mid-town real estate — in demand and scarce. It's only a place to sleep. We'll be out and about most of the time."

She moved closer. "Hey, I'm only teasing. I wouldn't care if we stayed in a cave as long as you accomplish what you've set out to do. And I'm sure you will." She stroked his cheek, the rim of his ear. "I believe in you."

His eyes darkened, his lips parted, and she was in his arms. His mouth covered hers as a man starved for nourishment and she gave herself freely, gave herself to this one man she'd never forgotten. Together, they tore off the bedspread and found each other, undressed each other. Explored each other until there was no more time, until their pleasure surged from within.

Afterward, she couldn't move. "My limbs are like burst balloons," she whispered. "Weak."

"Mine, too. It's like the poet said — a dream deferred. Remember? Langston Hughes?"

"Uh…?"

"When a dream is deferred again and again…it will eventually explode. It's a perfect analogy for us."

He rolled on his side and turned her head toward him. "You are the best of me, Jennifer Delaney. I've never stopped loving you, and this I promise — no one will ever love you more than I do."

Her tears flowed, and he covered her mouth gently with his fingers. "You don't have to say anything. Your heart still hasn't caught up to that beautiful head of yours."

She hated herself, she hated that he was right. "You once said you knew me better than I know myself. Maybe that's why you don't give up. I did date other guys, Doug, but…" She shook her head. "I never got too involved."

"You were waiting for me."

Her Doug had a huge romantic streak. "Nope. Sorry." She brushed back his usual hank of hair from his forehead, then turned her face into the pillow. "I wasn't waiting, Doug. In fact, I tried to forget you. Loving and losing is hard even when accepting half the blame, so I sure wasn't ready to jump back into the fray with someone else."

"I felt exactly the same way, Jen. But now I'm willing to fight for my happiness. What about you?"

##

She put the question behind her the next day as she made her way to Radio City Music Hall. Doug had told her that morning, "Go have fun. Be a tourist. Take a bite of the apple!"

"Oh, for goodness sake. You sound like a promo for New York. You can do better than that." She waved and disappeared, promising to meet him back at the hotel by five.

In ten minutes, the rhythm of the city crept into her feet. In another ten minutes, the cacophony of erratic sounds became a new musical fusion. Car horns, the patter of feet, bus belches, people's voices, traffic cop whistles, running motors. She hummed to herself as she walked toward her destination, and hours later, was still humming when she headed back to the hotel. She heard the shower when she let herself in.

"I'm home," she called out.

"Beautiful words," came the reply. "Be right there."

"It was a joke!"

Home? Jen scanned the tiny room, her tote and purse now on the desk, her shoes off and near the bed, a newspaper lying around on a chair and Doug's belt, wallet and sundries strewn. Messy, but almost comfortable. Did it feel like a home? "Don't get so dramatic," she mumbled, stretching out on the bed.

Doug appeared a minute later, wrapped in a towel. He leaned over and kissed her. "So, tell me all."

She felt herself smile as she thought back. "I am definitely an A-1 tourist! Radio City was amazing. I even paid to be part of a small private tour. Rehearsal halls, dressing rooms, even the lighting booth and projection room. And the Art-Deco — the grand foyer — really deserves an Oh-My-God! And that's what kept coming out of my mouth the whole time. So much fun."

"Yep. You're an A-1 tourist," he began while pulling on his pants, "who could be spotted a mile away with her eyes looking skyward instead of around her."

"Oh, stop. I was perfectly safe. And then I saw a show."

He paused to look at her. "Really?"

"Just lucky. I stumbled onto the half-price ticket booth for same day shows, and suddenly, I was Carol King."

"Ah-h. *Beautiful.* Perfect choice for you. You're sure beautiful to me."

Ignoring his compliment, she swung her legs over the side of the bed and stood. "I loved it, but 'perfect' would have been if you were with me. I had no one to share my pleasure with."

He kissed her once more. "Sweetheart, I would have seen it again just for you."

"Again?"

"Sure. I've seen many productions. I need to feel what's out there, not just read about it."

"And here I thought writers sat in their garrets and imagined stuff."

He shook his head. "Jennifer, Jennifer, Jennifer. I expect more from you. You'll soon see that we need to live in the real world if we want to connect with an audience. An audience is people!"

She waved and disappeared into bathroom. "My turn in here. Oh, I forgot to ask. How was your day?" God, she sounded like a caring wife.

"I'll tell you later. Just stay in your happy mood."

Uh-oh. She didn't like the sound of that.

##

A sage green sleeveless dress, strappy sandals and dangling earrings. Jen checked herself in the bathroom mirror and gave her hair one last brush stroke. Redheads always looked good in green, and auburn hair fell into that category. Ready for the evening, curious to meet Doug's friends, she was satisfied she'd hold her own.

"Okay, I'm rea—

He was on the phone but looked up when she spoke. His eyes shone and he emitted a low whistle as he talked back into the receiver. "Can't wait for you to meet her, Steve. And you'll be my second pair of ears at dinner with these producers." He disconnected and let his gaze travel from her head to her feet. "I should ask you to stay here until showtime. No one will be able to concentrate on anything but you. I know I won't!"

She felt heat rise to her face—which had probably turned pink. Something that never happened at work even after receiving a compliment. "I didn't want to let you down — meeting your high-toned friends and all."

"No more high-toned than we are, sweetie. Except...

She tilted her head and waited.

...the evening is turning into a business meeting."

"How did that happen?" She put up her hand. "No, don't answer. Let's go back a bit. How was the new lead for *The Broken Circle?* I thought she was the one question on your mind."

"A real pro. She did interpret the role a bit differently, but it fit. Staging a play is collaborative, Jen. I had to learn that. I thought the writer was king."

"You should be. Without you, they have nothing!"

He wrapped his arms around her and held tight. "It's great having you in my corner, but everyone brings something to the table. Today, the new lead brought her own insights and emotions. And that's how she'll make the part hers."

"Got it. It's interpretation. Just like me singing a song differently from another singer."

"Exactly." He glanced at his watch. "Ready to go?"

"Not so fast. So why is dinner turning into a business meeting?"

He stepped back and started to pace. "Two producers are joining us for the meal and to see *The*

Broken Circle—again. They're brothers, and they like my work. I-I was really productive during my residency here, and they kept their eyes on some of us." He pivoted to her and stood still. "They've got some strong backers—investors— and might be coming to Boston to see *The Sanctuary.*"

Sucker-punched. Her brain went into overdrive, and she swallowed hard. "So we've been living in make-believe land." She pulled a tissue from the dispenser and balled it in her hand. "It's happening again. Boston, New York. It always comes back to choices. Been there, done that." She pointed to him, then to herself.

"Not true. My home is in Boston with you. Nothing's changed. As you like to remind me, I can write anywhere."

But he'd said staging a play was a collaboration. And building his career seemed all about relationships. Actors, producers, directors. Producers were critical— they brought the money people. New York City, she had to concede, was the mecca for this whole gang.

And he'd walked away from it—for her!

Now she needed the tissue to blot her face, but her face was against Doug's shirt. "They're going to love *The Sanctuary,*" she said between hiccups.

"Not as much as I love you, Jen," he said, his voice hoarse. "Don't you know that?"

She did. She really did. She'd felt his love for her every day, but hadn't trusted it. Hadn't trusted them.

"But your career…."

"We'll figure it out. Okay?"

Her tears rolled faster as she held him tight. "I've missed you so much, my love. We have to figure it out because I can't lose you again." She leaned back and cupped his face with her hands. "I love you, Douglas Collins. I-I wasn't ready back then, but now…I think you're right. How hard can it be? After all, New York's almost next door to home."

##

She liked Steve Kantor immediately. She felt comfortable with him, as if they'd known each other for a long time. He sat on one side of her with Doug on the other, at the round table in a nearby Italian restaurant. Maybe it was the man's easy manner, maybe it was because he had Doug's best interests in mind. Or maybe it was because he'd let her know that Italian cooking was his favorite, just as it was hers. Whatever the reasons, she was glad he was Doug's friend.

"Doug told me you've never met a number you didn't like," said Steve.

She smiled and sipped her wine. "Not quite. I don't like those red ones on a bottom line."

He shot a look at Doug. "Oh, she's good. Very good."

"One reason why I keep her around," Doug replied, his eyes gleaming at her.

"Enough," she said. "I think we're getting company."

Doug stood as the two producers joined them. Steve rose, too. Greetings were exchanged while Doug made introductions to the Silverman brothers—Alan and Jeff. The had quick smiles and outstretched hands.

"I'm looking forward to seeing your play again," said Alan, the taller one.

"I know your work," added Jeff. "I judged a lot of contests for Playwrights' House—still do—and you always scored in the top 2."

The man turned to Jen. "Are you familiar with the one-act he has running off-Broadway?"

"I know about it," Jen replied slowly.

"Well, that started as a student project."

Pride bubbled inside her, and she leaned forward. "And then he improved it until it got noticed. Doug's the best," she gushed, unable to stop herself. "His words come from his heart and his head. And the audience gets it. They walk away standing a little taller, feeling more fulfilled. They see the world in a new way."

"Are you a lawyer?" asked Alan, seeming genuinely curious, and breaking the silence that followed Jen's impulsive speech.

Heat rose to her face as she shook her head. "That would be my sister. She's the smart one."

Doug hooted. "Don't let her fool you. The five of them—the Delaneys—were born whip-smart." He tucked her hand in his. "But I got the best of the bunch."

"Oh-ho! So that's the way it is," replied the producer.

"That is the way it is," said Doug, quietly and with emphasis. "Come up to Boston in September, and you'll see her again. Dinner in the North End. The best Italian food in the world."

After placing orders with their server, the conversation became all business. The plot, the actors, the creative team of *The Sanctuary*. Doug would be hands-on through the run.

"*If* it runs the whole eight weeks."

Jen's fork stopped halfway to her mouth. She placed it back on her plate and avoiding Doug's eyes, focused on the once-amiable Alan Silverman, who'd asked about her law skills.

"It will," she said with confidence. "I'm extremely familiar with the Commonwealth Theater. I know the audiences. I know the people of Boston. Patrons come from all over the area. One month's run would be minimal. Two months will happen. Besides," she added, "my understanding is that the theater's literary management had no trouble funding the show. It's that good!" She leaned back in her chair. "But, as always, everyone's taste is different, and you'll have to judge for yourselves." She looked from one to the other. "I promise you a warm welcome to my adopted hometown."

"If she's not a lawyer, she shudda been…"

The producer glanced at Doug. "You're one lucky s.o.b. She's riding shotgun for you. And sticking close."

"I noticed," Doug said wryly. But although he smiled, he didn't look happy.

Several hours later, all concerns disappeared as the audience viewing *The Broken Circle* got to its feet, acknowledging the cast with long, sustained applause. Tears ran down Jen's face, a mix of grief and hope as she relished the satisfying ending. And she wondered how the new lead could possibly be better than the woman in the cast now. Fortunately, it wasn't her problem.

But maybe it was. If she and Doug were a real unit, they had to have each other's backs. At least, that's what she'd noticed about Mike and Lisa. It made sense.

Jen, Doug and the other three men walked slowly to the theater lobby. "I loved the college production," said Jen, turning toward Doug, "I cried then too— but this! It's so much better than my memories."

"Because the script was brought to life by professionals," said Steve. "Good actors can make anything sound great, but they can't turn a sow's ear into a silk purse." He turned to Doug and clapped him on the shoulder. "You are one talented son of a gun, with an understanding of the human condition that seems beyond your years."

"Thanks. Thank you all," said Doug, including the other two men, "I may look young on the outside, but inside…? My mom says I have an old soul."

Is that why he'd been able to see through her defenses years ago? Is that what gave him the confidence to come back without any promise from her?

"We're impressed," said Jeff Silverman. "I won't say otherwise. Tell your mom she raised a gifted son."

Alan shook Doug's hand. "We'll come to Boston to see the new play, but we'll be calling you tomorrow about this one. We have another idea. The drama, *Doubt,* played on Broadway for a year and a half. Your play is still going strong after two years. Now's the time to take it on tour."

She saw Doug's eyes widen, his brows lift. He'd been concentrating so hard on *The Sanctuary,* this possibility for *The Broken Circle* had taken him by surprise.

She had lots of questions, and her fingers itched for a calculator. Her work was cut out for her.

CHAPTER ELEVEN

Doug hoisted their overnight bags and put them into the trunk, then settled himself behind the wheel of his car. He glanced at Jen. "Seat belt on?"

"Yes," she replied with a yawn. "Can't believe I'm sleepy on a Sunday afternoon."

He could believe it. She'd been on the go non-stop since they'd arrived on Thursday and had been up late the evening before with her mind working overtime. "I'm told that being a tourist can be an exhausting occupation."

She grinned. "I loved that part."

He felt her hand on his arm and turned toward her. "Forgot something upstairs?"

"Nope, but I have a question. Why were you annoyed with me last night?"

So, she'd noticed. "For one thing, you sounded like my mother, bragging about her boy."

LINDA BARRETT

"So what? The only thing your mother and I have in common is that we both love you... Oh, I see. Embarrassing. I'll give you that. However---I know from experience that it's hard to brag about yourself without sounding like a total egotist. Therefore, you were lucky to have me around."

Quick answer, quick mind. And turning defense into offense. He waited to start the ignition. "Alan Silverman was right. You should have been a lawyer. And what was that bit about the Commonwealth's literary management?" he asked. "You know nothing about that. And it sounded like the start of a negotiation. Keep out of it. I can negotiate for myself."

And that would be a mistake for him. "No, you can't. Even Mike doesn't. And Lisa says anyone negotiating on their own has a fool for a client." Jen twisted in her seat. "Don't drive off yet. Just listen to me."

"I'm listening."

"You know how I am about not liking nasty surprises. I did my research at home on-line. A play doesn't get produced regionally without backing from the theater's literary management."

"Research? If you wanted to know something, why didn't you just ask me? Don't you trust me with the answers? With the truth?" He heard the dismay in his own voice. Back to trust. The one subject that could pierce his heart. "There are always uphill battles. Success doesn't come without financial risk." Funny, she'd never asked about his personal finances, and he'd kept discussions about his earnings pretty general.

"Doug, I'm sorry..."

He started the car and began to drive, but before Jen finished, his phone rang. "That's probably the Silverman Brothers," he said.

"Put the phone on speaker," Jen requested.

"No way." Jen was smart, but this business conversation was *his* business. Not hers.

"It's just that two sets of ears are better than one," she said. "Like in a doctor's office."

"What I know is that you're a terrier. I'll do it because I'm behind the wheel," said Doug, heading toward the street, "but try to stay quiet. Don't insert any more 'research' into the conversation."

"Sorry if I stepped on your toes. But as the man said last night, I'm riding shotgun for you. Business is business."

Doug glared at her and connected the call. Then saw her reach into her purse and pull out a pad and pen. Geez, she was taking notes. It was so like Jen, he started to laugh. What did he expect?

He didn't expect a tour of six cities, possible dates, lots of money put up by investors. The producers would hire a director and cast out of New York.

"I like what I hear so far," said Doug. "Can we continue this discussion tomorrow when I'm behind the desk and not behind the wheel?"

"You've got it," came the voice from the speaker. "And we'll work up some figures for you to consider."

"There's always that!" quipped Doug. "Writers need to make a living."

The call went silent, and in the car, Doug felt only his own racing heartbeat as the magnitude of the conversation hit him. He made a conscious effort to focus on traffic and allow his breathing to return to his normal rhythm. More possibilities than he could imagine had just been thrown at him.

"It's a bit overwhelming, isn't it?" asked Jen quietly. "Want to pull over for a few minutes and just take it all in?" He looked around and wondered where on earth he could do that. They were still trying to make their way out of Manhattan. She must have noticed, too.

"Oh, never mind, Doug. Just drive. You'll absorb the shock—or should I say, the shockingly good news."

"Don't count chickens. Two months ago, I had no idea something like this would happen," he said, continuing to make his way toward the West Side Highway. "But I think—I think true opportunity is presenting itself, and I'd be foolish not to follow through."

"I totally agree," Jen commented. "Go for it."

But she didn't understand the true nature of the business. If she judged from only this fortunate episode, it would give a false impression. "Listen up, Jen. I'm going to be straight with you. I work in a fickle business. You have to make hay while the sun shines and all those other trite sayings." But nothing was trite about the business. Deals were made or broken. Dreams were shattered on a whim.

"Taking advantage of an opportunity is totally logical," Jen said. "I've seen in business that some people actually fear success and turn their backs on it. But you're not one of them. You work harder than ten people. I-I think you were born to do this. Your stories are wonderful. So, I'm okay with your 'fickle business.'"

If she were any other woman, he'd totally buy in. But she was Jennifer Delaney, whose best friend was a calculator. "Who are you kidding?" he asked. "You like to plan. You balance your checkbook. You budget to the last dollar. My plans fluctuate. You can't trust them from month to month, season to season. My income fluctuates, too. Unless something fantastical happens, I'll never be successful the way your brother-in-law is. And that's the truth."

"Even Mike has no guarantee from season to season," said Jen. "Injuries can happen. He's getting older. Did you know that Lisa used to cover her eyes during a game — for at least half the time? She'd be happy if he ran a pharmacy like his brother! He was a science major in college, in addition to playing football."

Doug whistled softly. "I never knew any of that. He's living every boy's dream."

"He's living his own dream," she said, "just like you." She turned in her seat, her fingers tapping against her leg. "I've been thinking hard, Doug. I've looked, listened and tried to consider every angle I could. In the end, after this year passes and with being in such demand, I think you're going to have to be where the action is."

Silence filled the car. "Maybe. Maybe not," he replied, keeping his tone even. He would not accept a déjà vu experience from her. "What are you trying to tell me?"

"Living in New York is expensive, but living in two places is outrageous. So how are we planning to be in two cities at once?"

He loved the sweet sound of "we." The woman could make his head spin, put her nose where it didn't belong, and frustrate him almost to death, but she was on his side.

"Did you hear what you said, my sweet Henny-Penny?" he asked. "Are you with me all the way this time? All the way into the future?"

##

Behind her computer the next morning, Jen took a deep breath and began her day. A normal day. Checking her appointment list, planning strategies for her clients and settling into and enjoying her familiar routine. The weekend's events had to take a back seat now, which was almost too bad. She could still see Doug's smile in her mind's eye after she'd answered his question.

"Knock, knock," rang out a familiar voice. "I can't wait another second longer. How was New York? And don't tell me I'll be losing another friend."

Jen waved at Alexis, standing in the doorway. "A whirlwind. We were constantly on the go. But don't worry about losing me! Doug knows Boston's my home. If you're free for lunch, I can fill you in."

"You've got it." Alexis waved and was gone.

The phone rang. Jen saw Lisa's name on the readout. "Hey, I only have a minute. How are the babes?"

"Come for dinner tonight and see for yourself. I'm feeling a lot better now."

"Wonderful, Lis. See you later."

If her meals became focal points, she'd gain ten pounds in no time. Shaking her head and grinning to herself, Jen tried once again to review her first client's portfolio.

Her next phone call came an hour later, just after her first client had left but before her next one arrived. This time the display showed the name of her supervisor. She picked up the receiver and inked in a meeting at the end of the day before texting Lisa about being late that night. And then wondered what to expect from her boss. She was curious, but not too worried. She and the department head had a good, respectful relationship.

Instinct prevented her from mentioning her appointment to Alexis when they ate lunch. Instead, she just raved about Radio City and seeing Doug's play. "It really is wonderful, Lex. And I'm not the only one raving about Doug. You should have heard the audience's applause."

"Oh, I did," replied her friend with a straight face. "And I never left Boston!"

Jen hooted with laughter. "I have it bad, huh?"

Alexis remained quiet for a moment, then tilted her head and peered at her. "Yeah, I think you do have it bad, but is that good? Doug's a nice guy, Jen. We all like him. And I know it's not my business, but you've got some history together. I saw your reaction when he showed up out of the blue. What was it? Only five or six weeks ago? It's happening kind of fast, don't you think?"

Jen stomach tensed. She broke eye contact and looked away. "I know his soul," she said softy, "and that's enough."

Silence beat against her ears for a moment.

"Then I'm sorry," said Alexis. "You're my friend and I care about you. I just don't want you to be hurt again."

Fair enough. "Don't worry about me. I even know how he earns a living in that crazy, creative business."

"Okay, then! That's great. I hope he's managed to save some of those royalties."

Suddenly, the practical, formidable, and financially astute Jennifer Delaney realized she'd never even asked him.

##

"Brianna looks wonderful! I bet she gained a whole pound over the weekend." Jen reached for the baby, happy to see Lisa's beaming expression and Mike's welcome smile, and bubbling inside with good news to share with them.

"Glad to see you, Jenny," said Mike. "We could use another adult around here, even for a short visit."

"Mike! I'm doing fine now," protested his wife.

"We'll let Jenny be the judge," he said, turning toward Jen. "Finally, Lisa's agreed to your idea of a night nurse coming in for a while, and we've made some calls. We'll have help starting tomorrow night for however long it takes our little girl to stop getting her timing mixed up!"

Jen looked harder at her sister. Underneath the smile and the makeup, dark circles hid around her eyes. "You need to get back to yourself, Lis, and nothing does that as well as a good night's sleep."

"You sound like a TV ad for sleeping pills or something," grumbled Lisa.

Maybe she did. So what? "Just telling you the truth. Besides, Bobby needs a mom who can run around with him, don't you, sweetheart?"

"Yup. But I got you and Daddy. He runs fast, but he can't catch me." The little boy took off down the hall, with Mike pacing himself in pursuit.

"He's a good dad," said Jen. "But the action never really stops, does it?" Her glance traveled down to the baby, and she leaned in and inhaled. "Ooh, that baby aroma. Brianna smells so good."

"When you've got the right end." Lisa smiled quickly before sinking into a kitchen chair. "I've ordered pizza. Not a great dinner, but that's what we're having."

"No complaints," said Jen. "I just wanted to visit."

"I'm glad you're here. I-I am a bit concerned. Mike's pre-season is around the corner, and then, a new NFL season starts the beginning of September. He'll be gone half the time, and Brianna's so much harder than Bobby was. It takes almost an entire hour to feed her. I get scared just thinking about it all. And then my career. But I need to get back to work or I'll have to start building a practice all over again. I don't know how I'll handle everything."

Jennifer shivered, then breathed deeply. Her strong sister needed some help. Jen's weekend with Doug seemed like a million years ago. And the recent conversation with her boss that had netted a promotion for her... was not something to bring up now.

Lisa reached for her hand, and Jen met her gaze. "I wish — oh, how I wish Mom and Dad were still here."

Jen's eyes closed. Tears threatened, but she swallowed them. Was there a time limit on grief? Commiseration was not what Lisa needed right now.

"We all do, Lisa. But they're not. So, listen to me." Maybe her tone of voice did the trick, but her sister remained quiet, waiting.

"I hate to say this," Jen began, "but sometimes you're your own worst enemy. I'm glad the nurse will be here tomorrow, but with all the demands on you, you'll need more help. Mike's parents can't live with you. They still work, and besides, they have lives of their own." She took a breath and slowly said, "You can't fight the idea anymore. You need to hire a nanny. A good one this time."

Lisa's horrified expression said it all. "Another one who won't work out? Nannies, schmannies! Besides, I - I'm not a society lady! We don't come from that world, no matter how much my husband earns. Mom raised five by herself. And I'm having trouble with two."

With the baby in one arm, Jen wrapped her other around her sibling. "You're not thinking straight, and you don't have to do anything right now except get some sleep. All those hormones are going wacky inside you. That's what all this is." Jen hoped her babble was on target.

"Maybe you're right," said Lisa, seemingly in control once more. "Mike says the same thing. And I still have some time. In another two months, Brianna will have figured out night from day, and we'll all get some sleep." She smiled a genuine smile, and Jen relaxed.

"We'll start with the nurse, and then we'll see," continued Lisa. "I'm so glad you live nearby, Jen. What would I do without my backup quarterback?"

Jen forced a wide smile. For the very first time in her life, being so needed by her family left her with a sinking feeling.

"I would have told her about our weekend, but really, she had all she could do to keep from crying while I was there." Jen lay back on her pillows, phone to her ear, glad to share her evening with Doug.

"Phew! I have absolutely no experience with this stuff," he said. "I guess you just have to punt. See what I mean about our imperfect world? Always a mixed bag."

"The good, the bad and the ugly. I suppose so."

"Only suppose? Your promotion is fantastic, Jen. Team Leader, soon to be Branch Manager. Fantastic! Too bad you couldn't share your good news with your family."

"Yes, but everyone at work will know when the memo goes out tomorrow. I'm a little nervous. I hope there's no backlash from the other consultants."

"They'll get over it. There's competition in every field. Enjoy the win."

She felt herself smile. "You're right. And now you're riding shotgun for me."

"Always. I'm not going anywhere."

"You're going everywhere! At least your plays are. Six cities?" she teased.

"I'm signing a good deal with the Silverman brothers."

"Did you ask for a share of box office? Even a small percentage?"

"Jen-ni-fer…" a slight warning note lined his voice.

"Just looking out for you," she said, "so get used to it. I did more research, and I take care of my peeps."

"And who takes care of you?"

That question hit with a force she couldn't have anticipated. The Delaneys took care of each other. Always had. But the foundation was shifting. Lisa and Mike were a unit, and the go-to people for her sibs. Jennifer was on her own. Independent, competent. Available to help when needed, but at day's end, alone in her apartment. She scanned the room, her gaze swerving downward. Alone in her bed, too. *So who did take care of her?*

"To be continued at another time," she said softly, before hanging up.

She'd considered them a team. They'd talked about a future, but had no concrete plans yet. Was it too soon?

Doubts crept into her mind. He'd never really shared his financial status with her. Those vague description of the playwrights' ups and downs didn't count. Had he been able to save any money in New York? And he certainly didn't want her input about business decisions. She didn't like secrets, couldn't live with them, and she'd tell him just that.

She shut the lights and closed her eyes, only to sit straight up again. Doug was not the only person keeping secrets. She hadn't shared one financial detail of her own success with him either. The realization stunned her. She fluffed up her pillow and slowly lay down again. Maybe they'd miscommunicated and were at a stalemate. Or maybe it was a matter of trust. She sighed. It seemed always to come back to that.

LINDA BARRETT

CHAPTER TWELVE

My dearest Doug — We enjoyed meeting Jennifer very much and would like to spend more time with you both. As you asked, I've enclosed Grandma's emerald ring with the highest hopes that you and Jennifer will be as happy as your grandparents were. Grandma believed the ring brought her luck! I think her luck was in meeting Grandpa. I'll be waiting for updates on your romance. Please call to let me know the ring arrived safely.

Love always,
Mom

P.S. I had it cleaned before I mailed it.

Doug smiled at his mom's postscript and felt the warmth of her presence from miles away. He held the ring up to the light, examining it from all angles and hoping Jen would find it as beautiful as he did. He remembered his grandmother wearing it all the time and saying that someday Doug would pass it on to his bride. Evie, she'd said, would want a symbol from her own husband in that far-off future. Well, his someday had arrived, and his real future would start now, if he could figure out the right time and place to propose. She wasn't getting away this time!

A romantic setting for sure. Maybe in Boston Gardens, or on a cruise in the harbor. Or maybe a fun day at the beach way out on Cape Cod. Behind a sand dune would provide some privacy. He wanted to come up with someplace special and memorable even when they looked back in fifty years. Nodding to himself, he placed the ring into his top drawer. A safe place until it rested on Jen's finger.

He sat back down at his computer, reviewed the last two acts of *Straight From the Heart* and sent it to Steve. His only novel was now a complete play. His buddy had seen the book version, so now he'd have a chance to comment on the stage version.

He ticked off the items on his project list. Rehearsals for *The Sanctuary* were going well. He'd made some good additions to his new playwriting curriculum for the university, and had bought a plane ticket to New York to see the new actress in her opening night of *The Broken Circle.* Picking up the phone, he called his mom about receiving the jewelry. To his surprise, she promptly announced plans to visit Boston the following weekend — the Fourth of July.

"Just overnight. Eve has a rare day off before the holiday, and we thought we'd see both of you—and Jennifer, too." His mom's excitement seemed mixed with anxiety.

"Are you sure Eve wouldn't rather sleep?" he teased.

"Don't joke. I'm actually concerned that she will. Those residents have a hard life. They really do."

"She loves it, Mom, but I'm sure she'll look forward to a little break with you and Dad. So where are you staying?"

"Well, that might be a problem," she said slowly. "Boston's brimming with tourists next weekend, and we're last minute. I've found nothing available yet, and I've made many calls. If my bad luck continues, I-I thought we could bunk in with you for one night. Eve has only a sofa."

"I know that sofa well." It wasn't a convertible one. He shrugged and offered his apartment, then thanked her again for sending the ring. After disconnecting, he texted Jen and got back to working on the curriculum. She'd call when she had time. Her promotion had come with additional responsibilities to go along with the additional salary, including supervising her entire. department.

He'd gone up to her office once when she was working late. Standing in the doorway, he'd watched, listened and admired her as she talked with clients on the phone. A perfect fit in her professional world. Some people might think he and Jen had nothing in common, but they'd be wrong. The theater was a business, too. Mutual respect for each other's efforts ranked high with him.

His phone rang, bringing him back to the present. "Are you up for another round with my folks?" he asked without preamble. "It's really about Eve…Yeah, I'm sure. I'm thinking dinner and a nice walk with a hundred thousand others to the Esplanade for the Pops concert. And I'll need to stay at your place that night."

He laughed at her response. Sleeping at Jen's was the easy part.

##

In her apartment a few evenings later, Jen placed her cell phone on an end table in her living room and looked at Doug, stretched out on the sofa. "Lisa and Mike want to join us tomorrow for dinner. We need to let them know where and when."

"With the kids?"

Jen felt a genuine smile emerge. "Uh-uh. She's actually happy with the nurse they hired. I hope the woman stays forever. Or that they hire a nanny again. Lisa sounds so much more relaxed."

"Then let the fun begin!" said Doug. "But you'd better tell Mike to wear a baseball cap...if he wants some privacy. Bostonians know their QB."

Jen waved his words aside. "No problem. The fans here are used to seeing him around town. He waves, nods and they leave him alone. He's got the whole thing worked out so he and Lisa can live like regular people—sort of."

"Regular people with a limo?" he quipped.

She walked over and sat at the edge of the cushion next to him, then brushed the lock of hair from his face. "Going out to dinner is a no-brainer at other times, but I'm wondering why they want to join us now. With all the tourists in town, it will be a madhouse wherever we go."

He studied her for a long moment before saying, "They think you're worth it."

"What do you...." The coin dropped. "Oh. They want to meet your family."

"Bingo."

She shrugged. "It's not necessary. I already know what I'm dealing with." She gave him a quick kiss on the cheek. "It could be worse."

His brows hiked up so high, she thought they'd touch the ceiling. Then he pulled her in for a kiss. "You never know with my father. Let's just wait and see."

She saw the doubts, a lifetime of hurt feelings, of perhaps being second-best. "It doesn't matter anymore, Doug."

"What are you talking about?"

"Your parents…Eve…history…"

"Hey, girlfriend. I only care how they treat you!"

She wrapped her arms around him, snuggled against his chest. "Love you, Doug. I'm a big girl and I'll be fine."

"We're like sardines in a can," grumbled Doug's dad as they made their way through Faneuil Hall Marketplace, the refurbished area of restaurants, food stalls and specialties, and probably the most popular tourist spot in town. "We'll never get a table anywhere here."

"We don't have to," said Doug. "Jen managed a reservation at Maguires, our usual place. With the city overflowing, she pulled a string or two. Now, we only wanted to show you around a bit. Can't you relax and just enjoy yourselves?"

Jen looked from Doug to his parents. They'd greeted her politely enough an hour ago at Doug's place, as did his sister. Now the other two women were walking side-by-side through the crowded outdoor venue, seemingly content with each other's company.

"Walking around here for 'a bit' is about all I can take," said Eddie. "We came only to visit with you and your sister."

"I have to admit," Helen chimed in, "that we've seen more people here in twenty minutes than we see in twenty days back home." An adorable grin crossed her face. "But it's fun. Look at the acrobats, right there." She pointed to the entertainers while Eve smiled at her brother. "I think Mom's enjoying herself."

"How about you, Evie?"

"Oh, yeah." She waved broadly. "This is so great. Being totally away from the hospital actually feels weird, but good. Oh, look—anyone want to play ping-pong?" She glanced over her shoulder.

"I'll take you on." Ed's eyes were on his daughter—his shining eyes— and a smile lit his face.

"And that's the way it is," Doug murmured to Jen.

Helen stepped closer to them as an enthusiastic five-minute ping-pong volley ensued. She cheered her family on.

"Reminds me of our ping-pong championships in the basement," she said, looking from Doug to Jen. "Great on bleak winter days when the kids were little, and the weather was abominable."

"Sounds like a nice pastime," said Jen.

"We drank hot chocolate and tried to make a little party of it, remember Doug?" She faced Jen again. "The winters in New England can be brutal."

"I'm well aware," said Jen. "I grew up in Woodhaven, not too far from you."

"Really? And now you're in the big city."

Jen felt her smile spread from ear to ear. "I totally love it!"

Helen looked at her son. "Well, she's a perfect match in that regard!"

Jen had rarely seen Doug embarrassed before, but now his face turned a deep pink. "Mom! Enough!"

She swallowed her grin as well as her own discomfort and changed the subject. "C'mon everyone. Let's start walking toward Maguire's. A slow walk, so Helen can see everything at the Marketplace."

Street performers, magicians, acrobats, musicians… Jen was glad of the distractions for Doug's family, and glad to have allowed enough time to arrive promptly at the restaurant.

Doug opened the front door. "Welcome to our Friday night hangout. Go right on in."

"Blessed air-conditioning," said Eddie. "Thank God."

Jennifer approached the hostess. "We're here on time!"

"How ya doing, Jennifer?" said the woman. "Your table's ready and the rest of your party's already seated." She leaned closer. "I didn't say a word about our favorite QB to anyone."

Jen high-fived her. "Is my favorite emcee here as well?" She scanned the room but couldn't see him.

"Oh, sure. Tony's here. We've got live music, too."

"He's making me work for my supper today!"

The woman shrugged. "That's life, but we all love it when you show up." She leaned in again. "You should hear some of the—well I wouldn't call them singers."

"Hmm…Doesn't matter. I guess karaoke is a draw for Maguire's. Good business decision."

"That's for sure. Follow me."

Mike and Lisa stood as they approached, and Jen elbowed Doug and nodded at her brother-in-law. Mike was, indeed, sporting a baseball cap.

"Incognito?" Jen asked, giving him a kiss on the cheek and then hugging her sister. "You look wonderful, Lis. The best yet since Brianna."

"Glad to be out and about," she said, extending her hand to Doug's mom and dad. "I'm Jen's sister, Lisa. And this is my husband, Mike."

Eddie looked from Jen to Lisa. "Sisters, huh? Yah…there's a resemblance."

"You can't fool DNA," said Doug as they all took their seats.

"And you look familiar," he said to Mike.

The quarterback shrugged. "Just one of those faces."

Jen never questioned Mike's desire to be low-key, especially when with the family, but she appreciated it that day. She suspected his motivation was for her sake. The rest of the introductions were made before Jen saw Tony heading their way. "Oops. He wants payback pretty quickly, it seems."

"Hi, folks," he said, "glad you made it." He homed in on Jen. "Are you ready? It's July 4th, so something patriotic to start, hmm? Come on, we've got a full house and more coming later."

"Later? Oh, no, Tony. I'm not staying all night. Besides, you've got a live band today, and from what I'm hearing, they sound pretty good."

He winked. "Only the best for Maguires. But I had to test the waters with you. Ya' don't know until you try."

"So, right," said Jen, waving him off. "I'll see you in a few." She glanced around the table. "How about we order some drinks first."

"Only a soda for me," said Eve, "with caffeine. I'm back on duty at midnight." She glanced at her folks. "Sorry. That's just the way it works."

Eddie leaned forward, glancing at Mike and Lisa. "She's a doctor, you know. Very smart. Works very hard."

"I'm sure you do," said Mike, addressing Eve. "Long hours are normal for some of us."

Eve's face brightened. "You're making me feel better. I'm not alone!"

Mike and Doug both smiled. "You can always call me at midnight," said her brother, "if you want to feel less lonesome. I'm usually at the computer."

"See, Eddie," said his wife, "we're the only ones here who are asleep at midnight!"

Their server approached, took their drink orders and gave Jen a heads-up from Tony. "Band's on break now, but they'll be back in five."

"Got it," said Jen, checking her watch.

"You said you sang a little," said Eddie, nodding. "Bet you can earn some nice change here. Tips and all. A social worker's salary can't be much."

The expressions on her sister and Mike's faces…priceless.

"Does anyone have duct-tape?" asked Doug in a quiet voice.

"I'm outta here," said Jen. "We'll straighten it out later." She leaned over to kiss Doug. "You can always stick him with the whole check," she whispered. "And order me a steak!"

"Genius."

"Start with something peppy and patriotic so that the diners can join in," said Tony, "but then switch to solos where they just listen. We don't want them to stop eating and drinking."

"Gotcha," said Jen. "Business is business with music on the side." Perfectly reasonable.

She looked at the band leader, gave him her key and a few titles she'd thought about in advance. "Can we do this?"

"Sure can."

She took the mic from Tony and welcomed the diners to join in singing *It's A Grand Old Flag*. What could be more patriotic than a George M. Cohan tune? Enthusiasm almost raised the roof.

"You did a fabulous job," said Jen to the happy audience at song's end. "You must all have had voice lessons sometime in your lives. Honestly, I couldn't have done it alone!" She bowed, waved, and invited them to sit back, eat, drink and relax while she celebrated some of the country's cities and states.

Looking at the band, she nodded and drifted into John Denver's *Take Me Home, Country Roads,* a celebration of West Virginia. The applause hadn't died down before she began Arlo Guthrie's *City of New Orleans.*

When she finished, she waved, blew a kiss, wished them a happy Fourth. And arrived back at her table in time to see salad being served.

"Better than ever," said Doug. "Every time, you always amaze me."

"I have a lot of fun," said Jen. She glanced at her sister. "Remember when…"

Lisa's hand went up like a traffic cop's. "Don't go there. I'm having a good day, no crying, no exhaustion. I don't want to look backward."

"You've got it," said Jen

"I don't know what any of you are talking about," said Eddie, turning toward his son, then looking directly at Jen. "But I do know that she's a keeper!" He paused a moment before saying, "Be fair now, Jennifer. You told us you 'sing a little.' Is that what you call *a little?*"

"Yup," she said, nodding. "It's a wonderful hobby. I enjoy it maybe because it's not my job. And…in all modesty…I guess I'm pretty good at it." She immediately felt heat creep up her neck. Her own fault. Since when did she compliment herself?

"Pretty good? You're great!" Doug's praises had her blushing harder.

"Lisa and I used to…." She stopped herself, glanced apologetically at her sister. "I forgot. Sorry."

The server appeared and removed the salad plates before Helen spoke up. "About the music — I imagine it's soothing after dealing with all the hard cases you must have. Homelessness, child protection…gosh, what area are you in?"

Jen ignored her family's stupefied expressions and glanced at Doug in appeal. He leaned toward his parents. "Let's step back a bit. You may have concluded that Jen's a social worker, but if you think back, she never claimed to be. What she said was, 'I help people, particularly with budgeting.' You both assumed social work was what she meant."

"Oh." A pink tint stained Helen's face.

"Well then, why the mystery? What do you do for a living?" Eddie's confusion reinforced his wife's.

Jen took a deep breath. "I do help people," she said. "Just in a different way. I help them manage their money." She waved toward the door. "In a building not too from here. Fidelity Investments."

The silence around the table was broken by Eddie's deep laughter. "Financial consultant! Oh, boy." He pointed at his son. "Good work. I said it before, this one's a keeper. You picked a real winner who'll help you stay out of trouble."

##

His father's words crashed against Doug's ears and tore his last nerve. He flew to his feet and loomed over the man. "You listen up, Ed Collins, and listen well. You may not believe this, but I'm making a good living as a playwright.

"And as for Jennifer, she was a keeper from the first moment I saw her. From the time she was eighteen.

From the time I read her first essay and saw into her heart. She's not only smart, she's beautiful inside and out. Why do you think I came back to Boston? She's everything I want and everything any sane man would want for a lifetime, would want for...a wife."

His voice dropped to a whisper, and he spun toward Jen. Tears were running down her cheeks, and he caught them with shaking fingers. "Oh, my God, Jen. I love you so much. I wanted it to be romantic, on a cruise, or at the beach, but—" He gazed blindly from side to side, unfocused on everything but the woman in front of him.

"Jennifer..." he whispered like a prayer, "will you..."

"Yes! Yes!" Her arms came around his neck and in the tiny space between tables he picked her up, never breaking his glance until he kissed her—-finally—before lowering her to the ground.

He felt her arm around him while she sought her sister's eyes across the table. But Lisa and Mike were already coming over, hugging, kissing, shaking hands with him.

"Welcome to the family," said Mike. "I couldn't be happier...because Jen is happy. Make sure she stays that way."

Doug studied the other man's features. His last words carried more concern than threat. "I will do my very best."

"Despite the legal definitions," Mike continued, "I've been *in loco parentis* since she was sixteen...."

"Thank you for that," said Doug. "It couldn't have been easy, but you did a magnificent job. She's perfect."

"Now that's a man in love!" Mike laughed and gathered his wife to him. "Looks like we have a wedding to plan."

Lisa stood on tiptoe and kissed her husband. "You mean, Jen and Doug have a wedding to plan."

"Plan is the word," said Doug, shaking his head. "You're off the hook on this one. But who knew that Maguires would be…"

"Perfect," said Jen. "Good memories here, and you just added to them."

A deep voice added, "You should thank me, son. Without me, you'd still be hemming and hawing."

"Get the duct-tape," sighed Doug.

"My father can be…ah…trying at times." Evie leaned over to kiss Jen. "I'm so glad about this. Doug's never looked happier. And that you're right here in town is great. If I ever have five minutes again…"

"Absolutely," said Jen, glancing at Lisa. "We know how to do sisters, don't we?"

"We certainly do. Welcome to the family, Eve."

Maybe if the best-laid plans often went astray, they left room for the unexpected events to work out well. Doug had no complaints as they made their way to the Charles River Esplanade for the concert. Jennifer's hand was snuggled in his, and he supposed they had a pair of dopey smiles on their faces.

"Hey, Jen?

"Yes?"

"Independence Day, huh?"

Her delightful laugh sprinkled the air, and Doug wanted to capture it forever. And he would. With the rough patches behind them, the road ahead would no doubt be smooth.

CHAPTER THIRTEEN

Jen had never been happier. The weeks since the momentous holiday weekend seemed to fly by and all too soon, summer was in her rear-view mirror. Emily came home from Tanglewood, the twins drove back to Florida and their junior year at school. Mike's NFL season had started, and baby Brianna continued to grow and thrive while her big brother, Bobby, started pre-school. Most importantly, Doug's new play would be premiered in a week.

To his dismay, she'd started a scrapbook for his work, cutting out the print ads and printing out the on-line ads promoting *The Sanctuary*. Sitting at her kitchen table on the first Sunday evening of September, she adhered the latest promo onto a page in the album.

"The boys used to keep a scrapbook for Mike when they were little," she said. "Maybe they still do. Or maybe Lisa's taken over. It kept the kids focused on something fun."

"It's keeping you focused on nonsense," he complained. "One sample ad is enough. Let's hope you'll have some good reviews to save soon."

The poor guy was as jittery as a bride the day before her wedding. She smiled, then stood to give him a kiss, sneaking a glance at the vintage emerald ring on her finger. A gorgeous piece that fit her perfectly. The family connection to Doug's grandmother wasn't lost on her either. The man had simply loved his grandma.

"It's beautiful," she'd whispered when he put it on her finger.

"But not more beautiful than you," he'd said, before emitting a big sigh. "I-I wasn't sure…it's not the usual thing."

She smiled at the memory and refocused on the job at hand. "I will have many good reviews to save," she said. "The play is wonderful. The cast is excellent. Tickets are selling…"

"…and I'm kissing the woman I love."

She relaxed against him, relishing the firmness of his arms around her, and still amazed at what a difference one summer could make in her life. "And then I'll take photos of everything I saved," she continued, "and create a real book. There are on-line services that do that. Each play can have its own album."

"Got it all figured out, huh? Love your positive thinking, honey, but there are bound to be flops along the way. You won't like creating souvenirs for those plays."

"So I won't!" She grinned and took a step back. "I understand that success can be a sometime thing in your world, so make hay while you can. We'll never starve, Doug. I've seen that you're not a spendthrift, and you know I love my career. I can't see ever giving it up, so we'll have that income to depend on."

She felt his pause. "What about kids, Jen? We've never even discussed having a family."

"Kids?" she asked, totally flabbergasted. "I am so not ready! I barely have enough time to help with my own sisters and brothers! Ask me again later on—like w-a-y later on. In the meantime, you can keep giving birth to new plays."

His laughter warmed her heart. "That I will, Henny Penny. I certainly will."

"I'm so glad you had the gumption to come back to Boston...to come home."

He cupped her face, raised her chin. "How could I not? My heart was here."

Now she knew that it was true. "I think mine had gone into hiding."

"Nah...more like hibernation."

She eyed him, blinked coquettishly and vamped. "Just waiting for my prince to come along and awaken me?"

"Exactly!" He swung her around. "A romantic fairy tale where at least we get a happy ending."

An idea sprouted. "Doug! Why not write a love story? If you happen to get a good idea, it would show another side of you. And if it were comedic...with a great cast? I'll bet Broadway audiences would go for it."

His jaw dropped a little and he nodded, regarding her seriously. "I've considered a love story. I'll let you know."

"Good. I'm glad I can contribute something to you, even if it's only a little idea."

##

After hugs and exclamations of welcome for Liz and Matt. Jen sat down for lunch with her former office buddies. Evan and Alexis completed the group.

"You two look great," said Jen. "Tell us everything about Kentucky."

Liz glanced at her fiancé, her cheeks pinking up. "Well…life is good. I'm working again, and you'll all be invited to a wedding at Christmas time!"

Congratulations echoed around the table.

"So you'll be back," said Jen. She reached for her friends' hands and squeezed them both. "So glad."

"But that's where it ends for a while," said Matt. "Actually, Kentucky's been great. Different—it takes some getting used to after Boston, but it's all good."

"Any new place would take getting used to," said Alexis.

"That's what I tell myself," said Liz. "At least I'm working now. But making friends is taking time, and with no family around, Sunday can be a pretty long day."

"We're still newcomers, but we're looking forward to planting some roots."

If Jen's stomach wasn't already knotted in anticipation of Doug's play's opening the next night, it would have formed a big knot then. Planting roots halfway across the country? No family nearby? She pasted a smile on her face.

"You are wonderful people—friendly and smart. I'm sure you'll be very happy sooner rather than later. But don't think new friends can replace us!" She leaned forward, and in a stage-whisper added, "You never forget you first love…s."

With that remark and ensuing laughter, conversation became general, as though the couple had never left town.

"Sorry Doug couldn't join us for lunch," said Matt. "He must be busy with last-minute details."

"And as on-edge as the proverbial cat on a hot tin roof," said Jen. "We just watched the movie on television last week, and it was powerful." She gazed around the table. "So I'm staying far away from Doug, at least, until tonight."

Head nods, remarks of understanding followed, until Liz said, "We are really happy about you and Doug, and we're dying to see your ring. C'mon, are you wearing it or is it getting fitted or something?"

Slowly, Jen held out her left hand, showing her emerald. "Turns out I love the guy. I'm even getting used to the idea of spending time in New York. It-It's not that far after all."

"Whoa-a-a-a!" said Matt. "We...never said it was. "But you? Wow."

"Yeah," she whispered. "A leap of faith with the right partner...my mom's advice."

She caught the inquiring glances that passed among her friends. "Oh, stop that. My folks are still here." She patted her chest. "I want what they had."

"Then you'll get it," said Alexis. "I'm guessing you figured out that Doug needs Broadway."

"He can write anywhere, but...yes. And that reminds me— two producers will be in the audience tomorrow night. They're the ones who get the backers for a play. So, will you applaud until your hands sting, please?" She took a breath. "I don't know how Doug does what he does. I don't know how he puts up with the stress. But I did learn that playwriting is a business. And *that* part, I understand."

"Ouch," said Alexis. "My hands are stinging in advance."

Jen gave her a thumbs-up. "And we've got to get back to work. Oh, I almost forgot." She reached into her handbag. "Voila. Your tickets. I'll see you all again tomorrow night."

##

If Doug's nerves were not shot before the performance, they were beyond frazzled after intermission, when he noticed a dozen empty seats that had been occupied earlier. So not everyone returned for the second half. Not a good sign. He'd mingled with the crowd in the lobby a little earlier, trying to overhear comments. General chitchat was almost all he got, but reaction to the play seemed good. He laughed at a woman's warning, "...it's breaking my heart, but it *better* have a good ending."

Not to worry, Ma'am.

Half-a-dozen of his students surrounded him, effusive with compliments. At least they were a distraction. He comforted himself with the knowledge that Alan Silverman had returned. The producer nodded on the way back to his seat. "We'll talk later."

Would it be a good talk or bad? The anticipation was like waiting for a test result that would affect the rest of his life. Jen rushed by, bestowed a kiss, and whispered, "I love the story."

Very unbiased. It meant nothing. He'd told her to stay with their family and friends until afterwards, when they'd either celebrate or pick up the pieces.

What a way to make a living. Throwing himself out there for brutal criticism. Or applause.

He stood in the back of the theater, watching the second half with a critical eye. They'd all worked hard— the actors, director, producer—but he sensed something different from a Broadway production. Something lacking. He took a deep breath and kept watching, while his expectations fell.

To his surprise, the audience's reaction sustained a curtain call for the cast. A hometown thing? Support for regional theater? And then Jen was at his side, bestowing kisses.

"It was great, Doug. In my humble opinion, your story made the actors look good."

"I'm not sure...some people didn't return for the second act."

"Maybe they got sick or something. Smile! We all enjoyed it." She nodded at their crowd of family and friends making their way up the aisle. But his eyes were only on Silverman.

"C'mon, my man," said the producer, "let's go for a drink."

"Right after I visit backstage," said Doug. "They'll be waiting and wondering. We've been working together for months."

"They did a fine job," said Silverman. "But make no promises to them." He paused a moment.
"Traditionally, we cast in New York and take the play to a city or two in order to hone it, get the kinks out. Kiddo, you did it ass-backwards."

"I had my reasons," said Doug quietly.

Silverman's gaze passed from Doug to Jen and back. "Don't blame you a bit. So how about I'll wait for you here."

"And I'll take the gang to our usual watering spot," said Jen. "I don't want to be in the way."

Her quick smile, furrowed brow, and the question in her voice... Oh, she so wanted to stay. With a fond smile, Doug said, "And since when did good manners ever stop you?"

Her eyes popped open wider than dinner plates.

"Like a visit to the doctor, eh?" he said, reaching for her hand. "Hang out, and we'll catch up with the others later."

"Not us," said Mike. "I'm taking Lisa and Emily home. Babies don't appreciate their moms having late nights."

Emily approached and hugged Doug. "I bet you got lost in writing that," she whispered in his ear. "I'm glad I'm not the only one."

"As they say, Emily, it's a tough job, but someone has to do it." He squeezed her hand. "You're not alone, kiddo."

"Good."

He shook Mike's hand. "I feel lucky you had a bye week and could catch the show."

"Sometimes things work out. Good job. Touchdown." Waving, he and Lisa left the theater.

Liz and Matt came closer. "Unfortunately, we have a flight to catch in the morning," said Liz. "But we're so glad we came. We loved the play. I laughed and cried. Good luck with it and with…everything."

"See you at the wedding," said Jen, waving as they walked out the door.

"How about Alexis and I take your folks to Maguires and meet you there when you're ready?" asked Evan.

"I'll go, too," added Eve.

"Whew, that was fast," said Doug. "Give me a few minutes with the cast and we'll head out."

Ten minutes later, the three started toward the producer's downtown hotel. "Walking at night is almost as good as a drink in a dark bar," said Silverman. "Privacy on the street. So tell me what you saw tonight, Doug."

Strange question. "I'm not sure, to tell the truth. The audience seemed to like it, but…something…" He gestured impatiently. "It sort of didn't match what I was hearing in my head."

"Excellent answer," agreed Silverman. "I'm happy to say that your material was better than the interpretation. And that's what was off."

"But the actors worked so hard!" said Jennifer, stopping in mid-stride. "They knew every line."

"I'm sure they worked hard."

Doug tugged her hand. "What he's saying, Jen, is that the actors were not Broadway caliber. And the director didn't know how to pull more out of them."

Silverman broke in. "For example, substitute Glenn Close as the older woman. Think what she could bring to that part."

Doug understood immediately, but his mind was on one track. "So it's not the script! I couldn't put my finger on...And when some people didn't return for the second act..." He closed his eyes, his mind sorting out the numerous rehearsals. "Sorry for the rambling."

"So what you're saying is that we have a friendlier audience here who enjoyed it without Glenn Close," said Jen.

"And who paid a quarter of the price," said the producer.

Doug sensed Jen standing taller, on alert. "So, what exactly are you saying, Mr. Silverman?"

"I'm saying that I'll be making a lot of phone calls, and the first one will be to my brother. I'll also need a copy of the script."

Doug caught Jen's glance. In the light of the streetlamp, her eyes shone, the corners of her mouth rose, and he felt her exuberance in the air around them.

"Told you so," she bragged. "I knew all the time."

"Right," he said. "Enjoy the moment, but remember that a writer's life is a rollercoaster ride."

LINDA BARRETT

CHAPTER FOURTEEN

In a daze, Doug disconnected the call from Steve Kantor and tossed the cell phone onto his desk. A roller-coaster ride. He'd warned Jen, but even Doug could not have known how prophetic his warning would be. They'd both been euphoric with the Silverman brothers' plans to investigate a Broadway production of The Sanctuary. But this latest news…? A shocker.

He glanced at his watch, then rose, too restless and distracted now to keep working. Outside his window, sunlight cast long shadows. The maple trees that lined the street were almost bare, but for a few stubborn leaves still clinging to their branches.

Grabbing his jacket, he closed the door behind him, ran down the flight of stairs and stepped outdoors. Jen would be leaving work soon. On this crisp afternoon in October, he'd surprise her at her office building. He'd figure out what to say as he walked. All he had to do was come up with a monologue. Some comforting words so she wouldn't freak out.

Who was he kidding? Of course she'd freak out at the mention of Los Angeles. The timing couldn't be worse. She'd finally become comfortable with the need to commute to New York, to being part of his life there. Her current to-do list included finding a place to sublet in the city as well as planning a modest spring wedding. A big enough list when added to her career.

In what seemed like only moments, Doug reached his destination and began to pace, while keeping an eye on the heavy glass doors. As people started exiting, he sharpened his gaze until there, in the midst of a crowd, he spotted Jen. He could pick her out among millions just by the way she walked, how she tilted her head, her profile with the cute nose. He waved and approached her. Even in the dusk of evening, he saw her wide grin and answering wave. And then she was in his arms, jabbering her delight and asking questions.

"I guess you needed a break," she said, now slipping her arm through his.

"And you are the best excuse for one." He leaned over and kissed her quickly. "Let's walk and talk. I received…let's say…an unusual phone call."

She turned her head and lifted her face toward him. "Is something wrong? Is someone sick?"

"No, no. Nothing like that. I didn't mean to scare you. It's just that Steve called me from New York."

They resumed their stroll. "What about? Another play?"

"Sort of."

"Sort of? I think we've discovered that you don't write novels too well."

The woman could make him laugh. "Remember you once suggested that audiences might enjoy a love story?"

Her nose scrunched up as she thought about her answer. "Hmm…you're right. I remember throwing that idea around."

"Well, the truth is, I actually had written a love story, Jen. That story was the failed novel, which I later rewrote as a play." Feed her the facts little by little.

"Really?"

"Yeah, but I wasn't ready to talk about it with anyone. I sent the script to Steve just for some feedback."

"And that was the call you received today?"

He paused and turned her toward him. He needed to see her reaction. "Yes. The title is *Straight from the Heart.* Steve liked it enough to send it to a friend of his."

"Which one? I met quite a few of your theater friends when we were in the city."

The more Doug revealed, the more nervous he got. He wanted this opportunity, but he also wanted Jen's buy-in. His heart thumped hard, and his hand sweated in the cool of the evening. He tried to choose his words.

"Ahh…none of that bunch. This friend of Steve's wants to talk about converting it to a screenplay." He stopped talking to let the meaning resonate.

"A screenplay? In New York? I don't…

"…not New York."

They'd reached her building. "Let's go upstairs," he said. "I'll explain everything."

She twirled and her eyes met his. "California. You're talking about California. Screenplays get made into movies, don't they? Wow, Doug. You don't give me a chance to breathe."

"Well, take a deep breath now. Take several. It probably won't happen anyway." He took the key from her shaking hand. "Relax, Henny-Penny. Ninety-five percent of manuscripts don't make it through. And ninety-five percent of the ones optioned never make it to the screen. My little play is a needle in the haystack."

He watched her silently put her purse on the table and take off her coat. Her changes of expression told him her mind was racing as fast as a car at the Indy 500.

"But you're so excited. If it's a nothing chance, why are you so excited?"

Good question. Not an honorable answer. "Because, sweetheart, I think it's a compliment just to be asked to the ball. And it also looks great on my resume."

Now her eyes sparkled. "You mean it's good for your ego!"

"That, too." He beckoned to her, and she came, arms raised to wrap around him. "I love you, Jen. So very much."

"Make that times two."

"I know. And I also know you'll understand that I need to talk to Steve's connection in L.A. He's an agent who's setting up a meeting with some studio mucky-mucks. I don't even know which studio."

She plopped herself on the couch. "And I know you'll understand when I say I have a three thousand pound stomachache, one pound for every mile."

He could well believe that. "If any of my work winds up on the big screen, sweetheart, you'll never have to worry about budgeting again. We're talking about more money than Broadway could ever pay out with one play." And if that didn't win her over her, nothing he said could.

Her mouth opened and closed. Her head tilted back. "You've struck out. I don't worry about that anymore anyway."

##

In the morning, her first instinct was to call Lisa, but she stopped herself. She'd go to work as usual, focus on her clients as usual, supervise staff as usual. She'd cling to her routine as if it were a lifesaver. And perhaps it would prove to be.

Lunchtime presented a challenge. She could barely eat, and an hour of free time allowed her to think too much. *Don't dump this on Lisa.* Jen had thought Kentucky was an awful move for Liz and Matt. If they knew her predicament now, they'd laugh. Not that anything was settled. According to Doug, far from it. But he'd been having a pretty fantastic year. If this was a roller-coaster ride, he was still climbing high, with no bottom in sight.

How could she deny him?

But how could she deny herself the pleasure of family? They needed each other—in Boston. She'd made that clear to Doug, and she'd already compromised about New York. Wasn't that enough?

She went home with a headache. And got a bigger one when Doug told her, "I'm flying out next Thursday night to meet with the agent and discuss the story with the studio guys."

He worked fast. Too fast. "What about your teaching schedule?"

"I'll only miss Friday office hours. I'll take the red-eye Sunday night and be home in time for Monday classes. George is one of the best-connected people in Hollywood. We can't miss this opportunity, Jenny."

She began pacing. "Maybe you can't, but I can. Things are going so well for us now, Doug. We've figured out our lives. Broadway, Boston, Emily, Lisa and Mike and the twins and the babies. And even Eve. We have a plan. We have a path. You're breaking my heart. I wish your happiness didn't cause sadness for me." Her eyes filled, and she couldn't stop the tears. "Sorry." She grabbed a tissue and headed to the sofa.

A deep quiet followed. She could hear the tick of the wall clock nearby. She could hear Doug's soft voice.

"Then I'm not going. Sadness? You're the last person on earth who I'd want to hurt. I vote for both of us to be happy."

But she shook her head, logic taking over. "You have to go. I can't be responsible for a missed opportunity of that scope. And besides, decisions made in the heat of the moment are never good."

He gave a sharp nod. "Jenny, I guarantee that in the end, this will turn out to be simply an educational opportunity. I'm familiar with the industry, but I'll just learn about it better from the inside."

She shrugged. "Whatever."

"The worst response in the world."

##

She actually agreed with him. Her response had sounded childish, but it was the only thing she could produce while numb. Living with Doug was proving to be anything but calm.

The following Saturday morning, while Doug was away, she practiced with the chorus again, preparing for their annual winter concert. In the afternoon, she cleaned the apartment as though preparing for a military inspection. Not a speck of dust, not a crumb of bread dared to show itself. She changed linen, did laundry and reviewed her wardrobe. Maybe a shopping trip was in order.

She called Lisa. "Want to introduce Briana to the wonders of shopping with her mom and auntie?"

Lisa laughed. "Sounds great except for one thing."

"What's that?'

"Man, you're getting forgetful. The Riders are at home tomorrow. We expected you and Doug to join us. I planned to take the kids and pick you up on the way to the stadium. Actually, Luis will be driving."

Jen took a quick look at her calendar. Her sister was absolutely right. "I'll be ready, but Doug's away."

"New York?"

"Not this time. I'll fill you in tomorrow. No big deal." She tried to make her voice light and airy, but her sister knew her too well.

"Okay…for now. We'll figure it out tomorrow. Love you, Jen."

"Back at you, Lis."

She disconnected and fell back into a chair—a chair polished so brightly she could see her reflection in the wood. Two nights. He'd been away only two nights, and the place was so quiet. Too quiet. No jokes. No discussions, no one asking about her day. She missed him! True enough. But he made her nutsy. Somehow, he pushed her most sensitive buttons. What had happened to her calm, planned and ordered life, the life she'd enjoyed only six months ago?

Doug happened.

Together, they were strong. Together, with their arms around each other, that was bliss. That was safety. So good.

But this pick-up-and-go business? The lack of routine, always changing goals? So bad.

She called Lisa again. "One yes or no question, Lis, so listen hard. If Mike had been recruited by San Francisco or Kansas City or Miami…would you still have gone off with him? Packed us all up and moved?"

"Of course! Boston seemed a million miles from home anyway."

A memory stirred. "Thanks, Lis." Jen threw the phone on the table and ran to her bedroom closet. Up high, high on a shelf was her box of keepsakes. She pulled it down and peered inside, not pausing to examine the trinkets of the past, simply searching for that college notebook. The one with the essay Doug had referred to countless times, the essay he'd read aloud to their class in his clear, beautiful voice. She took a deep breath and skimmed:

Most journeys are measured in miles. My longest journey began and ended in the moment my parents died in an auto accident... In that moment, I left childhood behind and clawed my way up to adult status. At least I tried to. Lisa wasn't home, and the three younger kids ran to me first on that terrible, life-changing day. I held them close while we waited, and they clung to me like babies to their mother. They were too little to know that I was a baby, too.

They'd needed her! Needed her to survive. No wonder she felt guilty leaving them. She continued reading.

Although the distance between Woodhaven and Boston is one- hundred miles, I measure my journey in light years. The wounds of childhood still bleed and my journey continues.

She sat on the edge of her bed and re-read the last line. Her journey had continued and would continue. An exciting future beckoned. All she needed was to take that leap of faith with Doug. She browsed other essays. Geez, she'd been a mess. Why had Doug ever befriended her? What had he seen?

Laughter rose. The guy had already taken his leap of faith—with her!

She walked back into the living room and brushed her hand once more over her parents' portrait. "Thanks for the advice, Mom and Dad. It feels right."

##

"I slept on the plane, so now all I need is a quick shower and I'll go to work."

Jen could have stayed in his arms for the entire day, but she was dressed and ready to leave the apartment.

"We'll talk tonight," said Doug. "I hope you'll be happy."

"I hope we'll both be happy." She kissed him on the cheek and ran out the door. "Don't want to be late."

But she was late getting home that night. Doug had been cool with the delay when she'd warned him about it on the phone, and Jen had wondered about that. But as soon as she walked through the apartment door, she understood.

A white cloth and candles dressed the kitchen table. A wine glass sparkled at each place setting.

"As they say, timing is everything," said Doug, bending to kiss her. "You couldn't have chosen a better day to be delayed."

"What are we celebrating?" she asked, waving at the table, her heart beating fast. "A new job in Hollywood?"

He took a step and stared at her. "Not exactly. Unless you change my mind."

"I don't understand."

He poured the wine and handed her a glass. "A toast to you. To us." He raised his glass and she tapped it with hers.

"Yes. Definitely." She took a sip. "Now sit down and talk to me. Our phone conversations left me hanging. So if you don't want curiosity to kill this cat..."

His laughter rang out. "Never. First off, the meetings went well. George liked the play, and the studio is thinking about an option. I never would have gotten that far without Steve's connection to George. The man has clout. He's got a good eye for a story."

"Maybe he's a frustrated writer. Regardless, he's smart. He loved your work, and I'm not surprised." She beamed at him.

"Save that smile for later!" He kissed her quickly on the mouth. "The big thing is, Jen, if it happens—and this is the part you'll really like—the money I'd earn—well…with your investment savvy, you'd never worry about money again—even while married to a writer."

All humor faded. Her hands trembled, and she put her glass down. "But I'm not worried at all…"

He waved her words away. "There's other good stuff—like seeing my script transformed onto the big screen. Going to an opening…"

"Stop, Doug. Just stop. All this—this 'good stuff' as you say, doesn't match the expression on your face. You look worried. Unhappy. So I'll put you out of your misery. I think it's great. I'll go. I won't argue."

He stared at her incredulously and emitted a bark of laughter. "You'll go?"

"I said so."

He came around to her where she sat, grabbed another chair and took her hands. "Why?"

She felt the heat rise to her neck ad face. "I figured a few things out while you were gone." Her voice caught. "I figured out that the kids don't need me like they used to. More important, I discovered that home—our home—is wherever we are together." She leaned forward, wrapped her arms around his neck and kissed him with a renewed hunger. "You've always been the one." She tilted her head back and saw him blink quickly, his eyes moist.

"I am the luckiest man in the world." His voice was hoarse. "I love you, my Henny-Penny, from deep down in here." He tapped the left side of his chest.

"I know," she whispered, then sat up straight. "Now that we've got that resolved, let's plan.

Hmm…we'll probably stay put until the end of the semester. When do you think I should give my notice?"

He kissed her palm, then each of her fingers. "You don't."

"What? Can you work from home? Or commute on the red-eye? That would be great."

He rose and started pacing. "I didn't say that, but I also figured a few things out during the last several days." He sighed a deep sigh. "I-I guess it was a significant trip."

She took another sip of wine and waited.

"They-they really liked my work. They knew about *The Sanctuary,* too." He paused and took her hands. "And they talked to me about emulating Neil Simon."

She gulped, the wine almost choking her. "Plays and movies, New York and Los Angeles? *That* Neil Simon?"

He gave a sharp nod. "Yeah. The man who has a Broadway theater named for him."

"What a compliment! You should have been flattered."

"Frankly, I was overwhelmed. And a little uncomfortable. There are a thousand writers in L.A. who'd kill for a chance like that. Why me?"

"Because the other guys didn't write your script."

He was silent for a moment. "Yeah. The script. I need to tell you about the script."

"Okay. I'm listening."

He rubbed his hands together, started to explain, stopped, and started again. "The love story is based on us, Jen."

Sucker punched. "What do you mean, based on us? On what happened to my family with Lisa and Mike and the Riders…?"

But he was shaking his head. "Of course not. I fictionalized the family and the background. The only part that's true is the accident. If you don't like it…then it goes in the closet. I wrote it in New York, before I moved back. But if it gets produced anywhere, I want to have control over it. And I won't have that in Hollywood. A movie is truly a group effort."

He cleared his throat. "So, in the end, Jen, I turned them down. And I hope you're not upset about, you know… the money part."

Drowning. In over her head. The only thing she could think to ask was, "What did you call the story?"

He coughed. Squirmed a bit. "I-I hope you'll understand. The complete title is: *Straight from the Heart: A Love Story in Search of an Ending.*"

"Oh-h..." Of course, it fell into place. She squeezed her eyes shut and pictured Doug, living in New York, writing, tending bar, thinking about her. Not knowing, just hoping. Praying.

Standing on shaky legs, she stepped forward and caressed his cheeks. "Our love story began and will continue right here. As for Hollywood? Maybe next time, everything will work out."

His kiss was strong, sure and bold. "Raise your glass," he said. "Here's to our future—the Delany-Collins branch of the family."

"To new beginnings," she added, "and a never-boring, adventurous life—with the right person."

A leap of faith. She nodded toward the portrait in the living room and smiled.

The End

HELLO FROM LINDA

Dear Reader—

Thank you so much for choosing *Unforgettable,* the first story in my brand-new series, *No Ordinary Family.* I hope the story kept you turning the pages as Jennifer Delaney and Doug Collins found their way back to each other after a long separation.

One of Jennifer's younger twin brothers, Brian, is about to discover true love in the second book of the series, *Safe at Home.* See if this major league pitcher can pitch his case to Megan Ross who thinks he's a total screw-up. An excerpt from this story follows this letter to you.

You'll also find a second excerpt here which shines a light on why the Delaney siblings are *No Ordinary Family.* In *The Broken Circle,*—the book that started it all—you'll be introduced to the Delaney's in their growing up years where the spotlight is on Lisa and Mike's story.

If you enjoyed reading *Unforgettable,* please help others find it so they can discover Linda Barrett books, too. Here's what you can do:

- Write an honest review and post it on Amazon, Barnes & Noble, iBooks, Kobo or any of your favorite book sites. Short is good!
- Keep up with me at my website at: www.linda-barrett.com to find out about upcoming books.
- Sign up for my newsletter on my website.
- Tell your friends! Word of mouth is still the best way to share news about a book you've enjoyed.

I truly appreciate you help in getting the word out about *Unforgettable* and my other novels, which are listed below and available both electronically and in print.

Thank you very much for being a Linda Barrett fan. I truly appreciate you!

Best,
Linda

.

EXCERPT FROM
SAFE AT HOME
(NO ORDINARY FAMILY SERIES BOOK TWO)

An organized mess.

Megan Ross stood behind her desk and reviewed the colored folders, calendars, lists and the dozen printouts she'd need for the coming week. She preferred blending manual and electronic methods when creating her schedules. Each worked for her, and to succeed, planning ahead was key. She needed a road map to ensure the public events for the Houston Astro players were a success every time the men interacted with their fans and supporters. If they screwed up, she'd have to make it right with all involved. She'd done that in the past—but, fortunately, mishaps didn't often happen.

A majority of the athletes were professional in all aspects of their career. Including public relations. One or two, however... just overgrown boys. A pair of green eyes came to mind, and her mouth tightened in frustration. Brian Delaney had so much talent but was so undependable on and off the field. She never counted on him showing up for a planned event. He was just a guy riding on good looks and an arm—when he used it. She shook her head at the waste. If she ever stopped to think about what could go wrong in her job, she'd have a meltdown.

Chuckling and dismissing the idea, she sat in front of her computer and began filtering appearance requests. She loved working for the Astros, and she loved her position as Player Promotions and Events Coordinator. Adding to her good fortune was a recent opportunity for promotion to manager. More money, more responsibility. She'd updated her resume and thought she had a good shot. In her competitive world, however, she didn't count on it.

When her desk phone rang, she saw Dave Evans's name on the readout. The team manager. She and Dave had a good rapport, communicated well, but didn't often overlap in their functions. Curious, she picked up the receiver and leaned back in her chair.

"Hey, Megan — come on up to my office for a minute. We've got a little something for you, just up your alley."

"We? Okay, you've got my attention. I'll be right there."

In fact, she'd run. Cooperation and a positive attitude were the keys for a single mom to enjoy job security and support her son.

With a smile on her face and a laptop under her arm, Megan quickly made her way up one flight to the fifth floor of the building, historic Union Station, home of the Astros and Minute Maid Park. She waved to Carla Weston in the outer office and knocked on Dave's doorframe as his door was open. He waved her in.

"Scott and Rick are with us today," said Dave, nodding toward the general manager of the organization and the pitching coach.

"Now you've got me very curious," said Megan, after greeting the men and taking an available chair. She was also a bit concerned. Two of the men directly coached players, while the third reported to the owner of the team. She didn't fit in with this group.

"We're glad you could join us," began Dave.

"Well, of course." She looked from one face to the other. "None of you seem too happy, so…" She gulped, a horrible thought entering her mind. "Am I in some kind of trouble?"

They all spoke at once, but she was attuned to Dave's voice. "Not at all, Megan. In fact, just the opposite. We've got a little situation with the team."

"Not with the team, with a player," added Rick, the pitching coach.

"Which, of course, affects the team," added Dave, rubbing his lip, an action which Megan had seen over the years.

She leaned forward, focusing on these decision-makers. "So, what can I do to help?"

"And if that isn't the perfect opening," said Dave.

"It's your show," said Scott Cohen. "I'm here only to observe. And report back to Harold. The club is not just a business to him. The man loves the game and takes an interest in every player we've got."

She nodded. The team's owner was famous for caring about every part of the organization, including the players. Maybe especially the players. But she still didn't know where this conversation was heading.

Rick started pacing. "As I said, we've got a player…a lot of talent, but…" He shook his head. "I'm not getting through to him."

"Then something's wrong," said Megan, "and not with you. My ear is to the ground. The pitching lineup appreciates you."

A glance passed between the two managers. "Told ya' she'd have a notion about it," said Dave. "She played women's softball at University of Texas. On scholarship, too. Made a name for herself. She knows the game."

A lump took root in her stomach as a pair of sparkling green eyes again came to mind. She glanced from the pitching coach to Dave, the team manager. Might as well throw the elephant into the room.

"Brian Delaney," she said.

She had fun watching their jaws drop. "Why are you surprised? He's just as unreliable for public events as he is on the mound. I obviously have no clout with him and am certainly out of ideas. Sorry." She began to rise.

Dave held up his hand like a traffic cop, and she sat down again. "Brian Delaney is either brilliant or a screw-up on the mound."

True. She'd watched enough games to see both. But could a pro team afford to have a clown in the lineup? Three pair of eyes were on her. "What?" she asked. "What can I do about him?"

"We think it's an attitude thing. Not a skill thing." Dave steepled his hands, elbows on the desk. "We want you to…to be his handler for the rest of the season. Figure out what makes him tick, get him to show up for every practice." The man didn't look too happy himself when he met her eyes. "Megan, the boss upstairs has a gut feeling about the kid."

Feelings. The sport was built on feelings. And performance, of course. She preferred the statistics route herself. "With all due respect to Mr. Weber, Brian Delaney was drafted out of college, so he's not a kid anymore, at least not in a baseball sense. At this point, have you considered trading him? If he's a problem that doesn't want to be solved, you might as well cut the team's losses."

Dave shook his head and leaned toward her from across his desk. "We need him right now. After last night's game, we're down to three starters. Damn tendinitis! We're calling up two players from the minors, of course, so we have our roster of five starting pitchers. Delaney's one of that five and the only left-handed one we have." He paused, stood and slapped the desk. "I repeat, we need him, Megan. It's either now or never. Can we develop him into all that he can be on the mound, as well as help the team maintain an honorable standing in the league?"

She was being pulled under. Hope and frustration swirled through the air. Heck, they were all frustrated. But the men were looking at her for hope.

"No technical training involved," said Rick. "I'll handle that, but with you in my corner, we might get different results."

"I-I'm not a miracle worker."

Dave opened a top drawer. "Your resume's right here. You're smart. You've played the game, you majored in psychology and communications…"

She held up her hand. "But I'm not a psychologist. I just love the game! But speaking of…has he spoken with the shrink yet? Our sports doc is really good. He knows how a ball player's mind works."

Dave's eyes fell. "He won't go. Says he doesn't have a problem. He's doing his job."

She jumped from her seat. "He won't go? Just like that? For crying out loud, fine him! Maybe if he'd stop cruising the clubs every night and get some sleep, it would help. Does he think he's Babe Ruth? That guy caroused, but when he played ball—he played to win!"

Pacing now, she wondered why she'd allowed her own emotions to kick in. Was it because she hated to see wasted talent, or something else?

"He's paid fines twice already, without an argument," said Rick quietly. "He's an untapped keg of potential. If I only had the key to…" his voice trailed off.

"We've invested a ton of money in him," said Scott, the general manager. "Either he comes through or I'll recommend cutting him." His gaze touched on each of them. "My job is telling Harold the facts and providing a well thought-out opinion. In the end, he'll make up his own mind."

"We don't want to cut him." Dave said immediately. He glanced at Megan, then looked away, then back at her. "There's one thing he does like," he said.

"Oh?"

"Yeah. He likes women. And he likes you."

"Women? I can believe." But liking her? Impossible. Brian Delaney didn't know she was even alive. "If the players like me, it's because I speak their language, and I don't waste their time." Her voice softened. "And believe me, I take their camaraderie as a big compliment. In general, the guys trust me. They come through at the hospitals, charity events…"

The three men nodded in unison, and Megan fought to hold back a chuckle at the sight. Just for the moment. The situation, itself, was not funny at all.

"We have a hunch, Megan, that you can pull this off," said Dave. "Rick and I would totally support you."

She studied each man now. They weren't kidding around. She had her career to consider. The possible promotion. And her reputation as a professional within the organization. Of course, soon her resume would read: *baby-sitter to spoiled brat, Brian Delaney.*

"A hunch?" she repeated. "Well then, that's the bottom line in our world, isn't it? Hunches, feelings, superstitions, jinxes, aligned planets, auras, and lots of woo-woo." She smiled to include herself in the observation. "I've lived with those 'hunches' all my life, too. And that fool does have oodles of talent."

"So, you're in?" asked Dave.

"Let's hope his womanizing doesn't apply to me—or I'm out."

"Agreed."

"By the way," said Scott, "speaking of bottom lines. Did we mention the bonus that goes along with this special assignment?"

She sat taller. "I'm all ears, my friends." A single mom never turned down a chance to earn overtime.

"Ten thou for the try, and another fifteen for the get. If you turn him around, Megan Ross, that's twenty-five thousand beyond salary and holiday bonus." The general manager was speaking for the owner. It seemed everyone was as serious as death about this 'assignment.'

She slowly exhaled the breath she'd been holding. Their generosity was nothing to sneeze at. Her ex was totally out of the picture. A real charmer with no sense of responsibility. Not unlike Delaney, she supposed.

"We would have mentioned it earlier," said Dave. "But we all played the same hunch on you, and we all won." His grin stretched across his face.

She chuckled and shook her head. "Might have known." More than ever, she felt at one with the organization. She'd earned their respect before doing a day's work with Delaney. Now she'd have to retain it.

##

Brian Delaney glanced at his watch as he ran up the five
flights to Dave Evans's office. Three o'clock. And the
game started at 7:05 that night. He took a moment to
catch his breath at the top of the stairs, content with the
timeframe. He'd be able to make a prearranged visit at
the hospital and be back for pre-game warm up. After
last night's trouble with Travis Watson's arm, Brian
wanted to be in good form that night—for the team's
sake—in case they needed him. Actually, Brian felt
awful about Travis, too. No pitcher wanted to be laid up
with tendinitis. He'd come through for a friend.

He jogged to Dave's office, called out a "yo" to
Carla and stopped at the doorway to stare at the best pair
of legs in Houston. So glad she often wore sundresses!
Megan Ross not only had legs, she had a body, face and
a personality to boot. The total package. He enjoyed
rattling her.

"Hey, y'all," he said, after knocking on the door.
"Is it a party?" He turned to Megan. "Good to see
you...I think. Or am I in trouble again?" He paused.
"Was there a photo shoot or something I missed?"

"Nope," she said, shaking her head, blonde hair
swirling on her shoulders. "But we will be working
together. Why don't you have a seat?" She turned to
Dave. "You're up. Time to explain the plan."

Brian didn't like the look that passed between
them, didn't like the sound of the word "plan." And he
didn't like the four-to-one odds. He continued to stand
near the doorframe and leaned against the wall. His hand
went into a pocket of his baggy cargo shorts and cupped
one of the baseballs he always had with him. A habit
he'd acquired since moving to Houston.

As he listened to the "plan," he began to relax. It
had to be a joke. He waited until Dave ran out of steam.

"And to think, my ears weren't even burning as
you spent all this time talking about me," he began.

"Probably because you were just having fun. So, let's put it to rest. First of all, as lovely as Megan is, I don't need a baby-sitter. And second," he said, stepping further into the room, "baseball *is* about having fun! For the fans and the players."

If Dave Evans's eyes opened any wider, they'd pop out. "Do I look like I'm having fun?" the man growled.

"Well, maybe I can help you out there. Help you relax more." Brian took the ball out of his pocket, then reached for another and a third from the opposite pocket. He tossed one ball into the air, then added the second, then the last. For thirty seconds the room was silent as all eyes watched him juggle the three balls.

"God, his eye-hand coordination is fantastic," whispered Rick.

Brian smiled inside, kept juggling, and spoke. "I do take the game seriously. Check the stats. Don't I have the best record in the league for fewest stolen bases allowed?" Of course, he did. Catching runners was a hoot.

He heard mumbled agreement and juggled himself toward the door. "Sorry to break this up early, but I've got a date...with a very special lady." His heart squeezed for a moment as one by one, he caught each ball.

Turning at the doorway, he added, "I can't disappoint her." He jogged back to the stairwell.

Silence reigned for half-a-minute after Brian disappeared. Dave spoke first. "What just happened here? Does anyone know what just happened in here?"

"That was Brian being Brian," said Megan. "Doing what he always does—having fun."

"At whose expense?" asked Dave.

"And who's the special lady?" asked Megan. "Maybe she's the key to unlocking him."

"No girlfriends that I know of," said Rick. "And I'd probably know if there was someone."

"Ditto that," said Dave. "His whole family's back east though. His brother's with the Red Sox. Maybe we should've drafted him instead."

"We needed a pitcher, not a fielder," said Rick.

Interesting. She hadn't thought about his brother or his family, for that matter. She knew little about them, had never been curious. She knew the married players' wives and many of their children. They went to the games and most of the women played in the annual wives' softball game each year, which she coached. But as for the single guys…she didn't know much. They seemed more self-contained. Or maybe they just preferred keeping their private lives…private.

"I'll leave you three to figure out the details," said Scott, "and I'll brief Harold on our game plan." He turned to Megan. "Do your best, but don't make sacrifices you wouldn't ordinarily make."

"Huh?"

"You're part of the team, too, Megan. Play it safe." He waved and left the room.

"I'll second that. Delaney's a playboy, so keep your guard up," said Dave.

"You're concerned for nothing," said Megan. "I don't make the same mistakes twice."

"You've got a great kid, though," said Dave. "So that wasn't a mistake."

"My son," Megan began, and to her surprise, started choking up, "is the best child in the world." A new thought struck her about this assignment. "I need to keep Delaney away from Josh." She walked back and forth. "I'll have to figure out..."

Dave's hand went up again. "Slow down a minute. This whole project might not last very long at all. Think about Sandy Koufax. It took him six years — six years, Megan—before the whole game clicked for him and his brilliance on the mound showed up as no-hitters and perfect games. Brian Delaney is just about at that same point." He looked at her and shrugged his shoulders. "Maybe...?'

She tilted her head back. "From your mouth to God's ears, as my mom always says. With Delaney, we really will need divine help to perform an attitude adjustment or...should I say, a baseball miracle?"

"Ha! You're right. I hope you have a direct line to the bigger boss upstairs."

EXCERPT FROM
THE BROKEN CIRCLE
(NO ORDINARY FAMILY SERIES BOOK FIVE)

January 1995
Boston

A knock at her grad school apartment door pulled Lisa
Delaney away from Commonwealth of Massachusetts
vs. Torcelli Construction. Eyes burning, she rubbed her
lids while, from her iPod, she heard Bryan Adams insist
that everything he did, he did for her. Old song. Easy
words. If the man really wanted to impress, he could
take her contracts exam in the morning.

She pushed away from her desk, covered in law
books and case briefs, and rose from her chair,
stretching, bending and groaning. Her knees creaked like
an arthritic old lady's. Shaking her head, she emitted a

long sigh and promised herself a gym visit the next day—after the exam.

A second knock echoed, this time more impatiently

"I'm coming. Hang on." Nimble again, she rushed across the room and opened the door.

Her eyes widened, her stomach began to roil as she looked at two uniformed state troopers, snow melting on their jackets, cop faces in place. Her thoughts raced with possibilities. Classmates? Mike? Oh, please, not Mike.

"Are you Lisa Delaney?"

She stared at bad news and froze. All of her. Nothing worked. Not her mind, tongue, or breath. Perhaps her heart had stopped, too. One man coughed. The other repeated the question.

"I-I'm Lisa."

"Are your parents' names Robert and Grace Delaney?"

Oh, God, yes! Her heart raced at Mach speed, but she couldn't feel her legs at all. "What happened?"

"May we come in, Ms. Delaney?" Taller cop.

She nodded and pulled the door wider, but the knob slipped through her sweaty hands and she lost her balance.

"You might want to sit down."

As though moving underwater, she struggled into the closest chair.

"I'm afraid there's been an accident on the turnpike," began the quiet-till-now officer. "A fatal accident."

"Not...not my...my parents?" She barely got the words out before the officers' sympathetic silence answered her question.

"But that's impossible! I just spoke to my dad..."

"When was that, ma'am?"

When? When? "I think...maybe...last...last night...." Her voice drifted. Daddy had been checking up on his eldest, his numero uno child, joking with her about an apple a day. Staying healthy. A convenient excuse to call. To keep in touch with the one who'd left home. She'd understood his M.O. a month after arriving at school. Sweet, loving man. A man with a phone.

"Wh-what…?" Her throat closed.

The cops seemed to understand her intent. "The official investigation is ongoing, but according to preliminary reports, the other driver lost control of his vehicle and did a one-eighty."

"Drunk? But…but it's the middle of the week." As if that fact could change things.

"The driver's blood alcohol was normal."

"Then what…? The road…?"

"Icy conditions contributed. The temperature drops at night, and your folks were approaching at just the wrong moment. There were no survivors. I'm very sorry."

She nodded. *No survivors? Mom and Dad?* She wanted to cover her ears.

The other officer looked at his notes and said, "The Woodhaven police are with your brothers and sisters."

Oh, God, the kids… She had to get back to Woodhaven!

Standing quickly, she was hit by a wave of nausea and fell back into her chair. She doubled over, hand on her stomach. The phone rang, startling her further. She stared at the instrument, half-buried by textbooks, reached forward, and slowly lifted the receiver. "Hello?" she whispered.

"Lisa! Lisa! The police are here. Mom and Dad were in an accident. You have to come home! Now! I'm scared."

Jennifer. Her social butterfly teenage sister whose life revolved around boyfriends, best friends, and having fun. Except, not tonight. In the background, she heard the cacophony of younger voices crying and talking at the same time. She heard little Emily's high-pitched wail. "When is Lisa coming?"

"Hang on, Jen." She took a breath and looked at the officers. "There are four of them. Emily's only seven. My twin brothers are nine. Jen's sixteen. I've got to get there—a hundred miles—and I don't own a car." She couldn't afford one and didn't need one in a city with mass transit.

The troopers nodded, and she spoke into the phone again.

"I'll be there soon, Jen. As soon as I can. Maybe William and Irene can stay with you meanwhile." Her fiancé's parents lived across the street.

"They're not home. They went to Miami to see Mike play. Didn't you watch the game yesterday?"

"Of course I watched, but I didn't know his folks flew down." Mike had subbed for the starting quarterback and played an entire quarter. It was only his first year, but now the Riders were in the play-offs.

"So, Jen, you need to be in charge now until I get there. You and the kids sit tight and wait for me." She glanced toward the window, where falling snow was reflected by the light of the streetlamps.

"It might take a little while," she added. "It's a big trip, and the roads are bad…" What was she saying? Her parents had just been killed on those roads. "Jen, honey, let me talk to one of the officers there."

Her hand shook as she gave the receiver to the state cop. "Ask if they told the kids the truth."

In seconds, he shook his head. "Not yet. They're getting a social worker in on it."

She raised her eyes to his. "Please tell them not to do or say anything until I get there. Okay?"

Perspiration trickled from every pore. She shivered and sweated until finally her stomach lurched. Running into the bathroom, she vomited until nothing remained. Then she brushed her teeth, packed her suitcase to the brim, and snapped it shut. The sound focused her, and she inhaled a deep breath. *Be strong, be strong...*

One of the troopers held the door open. Her gaze skimmed the small apartment. She'd been happy there and ecstatic at being accepted into the program. She glanced at her textbooks before locking on to her college graduation photo. Her parents stood on either side of her, their smiles wide.

"Oh-h... One second." Her own future was now uncertain. Dropping her suitcase, she darted to the wall, took down the picture, and tucked it under her arm. Their dreams and her dreams might have to wait awhile.

#

Michael Brennan needed three days to get home to Woodhaven and to Lisa. It seemed like three years.

He tossed his luggage in his parents' front hall, turned around, and headed directly across the street. The Delaneys lived in a two-story wood-framed house with a front porch similar to his and to all the other homes on Hawthorne Street. He'd grown up there, but Lisa and her family had moved in over four years ago in June, right after her high school graduation. He'd graduated from a neighboring high school that same year. Their paths hadn't crossed until the evening his mother baked a cake and insisted their family welcome the new neighbors. Moaning and groaning, he'd given in, and the Brennans had gone to visit the Delaneys.

When Lisa opened the door and walked outside, he'd almost tripped up the front steps. One glance and he couldn't speak. His brain froze, too, as if a lightning bolt had slammed him head to toe. Big violet eyes, long, dark wavy hair, and a killer smile. A friendly smile. *Who wouldn't have fallen in love with her?* But he'd been the lucky one, the lucky guy who'd relished every single day since Lisa Delaney had first appeared at that front door.

Now her sidewalk needed shoveling. The streets had been plowed since the storm a few days ago, the walkways, too, but snow had fallen again yesterday, and surfaces had turned icy. He flexed his shoulders and entered the house. He'd take care of the snow after he wrapped his arms around her…if he could find her.

The Delaney house was packed. He recognized Lisa's aunts and uncles from out of -town, and all the neighbors, of course. Lisa's closest friends, Sandy and Gail, were there, too. Either they'd stayed all day or had just come from work. He waved and searched for his mom.

"Where's Lisa?"

"I'm glad you're here, Michael," she said, giving him a quick kiss, "but don't expect too much from Lisa. She's overwhelmed as…as we all are." Irene Brennan gazed up at the ceiling, indicating the second floor. "She's got the kids with her. The funeral's tomorrow, and she wants time alone with them."

"Alone doesn't include me."

He took the stairs two at a time, sensing the glances, the sympathy of the visitors as he made his way up. He appreciated their support, but they didn't have to worry. Surely, he could handle whatever he found. Surely, he and Lisa could handle it together.

He paused in the hallway at the top of the stairs. Each of the four bedroom doors stood ajar, but he could hear nothing. He started to push the first door open when, from the end of the corridor, he heard Lisa singing quietly, "Too-ra Loo-ra Loo-ra, Too-ra loo-ra lie…"

Was she trying to put the kids to sleep at five o'clock in the afternoon? He slowed his pace and walked the last few steps before knocking softly and entering the master bedroom. Lisa sat on her parents' bed, leaning against the headboard, the twins dozing on either side of her, little Emily sleeping on her lap. Jennifer lay across the foot of the bed, also sound asleep. He took it all in and understood that day and night had no meaning to them.

"Lisa..." A whispered prayer.

Her red-rimmed eyes brightened, her arms opened, and he was there. Kissing her and gently shifting one little brother lower on the mattress. She began to cry, her tears mingling with his as he rained kisses, and his tension melted simply by holding her in his arms. Tears flowed as he continued to embrace her and grieve while remembering Grace and Robert Delaney.

They'd been wonderful neighbors, wonderful parents, and good friends with his folks. The Delaneys had worked so hard to finally become "owners" instead of "renters," and celebrated their move to Hawthorne Street each time they'd made a mortgage payment. Lisa had told him how her dad would brandish the check and twirl Grace around the kitchen every single month. With their growing family, it had taken them fifteen years to afford their own home.

"How long can you stay?" Lisa whispered.

"He can't," mumbled nine-year-old Andy, rousing slightly. "He has to go to the conference championship game. And maybe to the Super Bowl."

"But not yet," Mike said, rubbing the boy's head with affection, but focusing his gaze on Lisa. "I'll be here for the funeral tomorrow. You won't be alone. Then I'll be back in a week. One short week." Which might feel like an eternity to Lisa.

"I'm glad, but-but everything has changed," she said, pulling a tissue from the nearby box and blotting her face. "We need to rethink our plans."

"The basics haven't changed," he replied quickly. "I love you, Lisa Delaney. And don't you forget it."

Her eyes shone. She pressed his hand, her fingers narrow and delicate around his broader ones. "I love you, too, but-but…." She sighed and glanced at the assorted children. "I'm not sure what's going to happen next," she said quietly.

"I am," he said. "I'm going to kiss you again."

And he did. When she kissed him back, when she lingered and leaned against him, he almost collapsed with relief. She was *the one* for him. No matter what. Her needs, the kids' needs….

"We'll sort it out when the time comes," he said. "I'll support you in every way I can." The logistics would no doubt be complicated, but he had faith that he and Lisa could do anything as long as they did it together.

She offered a wan smile. "I know you'll do your best, but you have commitments to the team. You're so talented! We all know you're being groomed as a starting quarterback, maybe even next year. So I think, for both our sakes, I need to handle this-this family situation by myself."

No, she didn't, but her brave effort tore a corner of his heart. "I think you're right about my place in the team," he said slowly, "but that's in our favor. The money's good." He'd worked hard with his coaches, and his natural talents had been recognized. His dream career loomed just over the horizon.

"I must be weird," said Lisa. "I never think about your salary. Even your first year minimum is like make-believe Monopoly money to me. It doesn't matter. I'm just so…so proud of you."

Men cry. Even big football players. But once that afternoon was enough. His throat ached as he swallowed to stem more tears. Lisa needed him to be strong.

"Have I ever told you about my conversation with your dad at the end of the summer you moved to Hawthorne Street?" he asked. "It was right before I went off to Ohio State on my scholarship."

"All Daddy told me was that you were too big for your britches, but he was laughing."

A surge of love and a wave of sadness—both raced through Mike. The words sounded exactly like something Rob Delaney would say. And the laughter– well, laughter was the norm in Lisa's family. Her dad loved to tell a good story and could imitate the comedy greats and their jokes. Rob had been a natural "on stage," and no one had a bigger heart.

"Before I left for college," Mike continued, "I told him I was going to marry you someday."

"You've got to be kidding! We were only eighteen. We'd just met that very summer." For a moment, her expression lightened. She tipped her head back, and her eyes met his. "And what did he say?"

"He said that I'd better treat you like gold— always. And I promised I would."

"O-o-h…." Despair once again etched her face. "Our lives… everything..."—she waved her arm— "has changed. I can't-I *won't* hold you to any promise."

"You have no vote." He kissed her again, vowing to keep that promise. Loving Lisa was the easy part. Building a solid future together…well, that goal might be more difficult to reach now. Lisa was in no condition to make any decisions. Their next steps would be decided by him.

His gaze rested on each of the youngsters, one at a time. Four sweet, innocent children. Without warning, his heart started to race, and his palms became covered in sweat. Fear. Like Lisa, he was almost twenty-three, and deep down, he was scared, too. He had no experience with kids, not even a younger brother or sister. But he wouldn't give himself away, wouldn't let Lisa know. A quarterback led with confidence on the field. Now he had to do the same at home.

LINDA BARRETT BOOKS

NOVELS—ROMANCE

No Ordinary Family Series
Unforgettable (Bk. 1)

Safe at Home (Bk. 2)

Heartstrings (Bk. 3)

His Greatest Catch (Bk. 4)

The Broken Circle (Bk. 5)

Starting Over Series

True-Blue Texan (Bk 1)

A Man of Honor (Bk. 2)

Love, Money and Amanda Shaw (Bk.3)

The Inn at Oak Creek (Bk.4)

Flying Solo Series

Summer at the Lake (Bk. 1)

Houseful of Strangers (Bk. 2)

Quarterback Daddy (Bk. 3)

The Apple Orchard (Bk. 4)

Pilgrim Cove Series

The House on the Beach (Bk. 1)

No Ordinary Summer (Bk. 2)

Reluctant Housemates (Bk. 3)

The Daughter He Never Knew (Bk. 4)

Sea View House Series

Her Long Walk Home (Bk. 1)

Her Picture-Perfect Family (Bk. 2)

Her Second-Chance Hero (Bk. 3)

NOVELS—WOMEN'S FICTION

The Broken Circle

The Soldier and the Rose

Family Interrupted

For Better or Worse – A boxed set of all three WF novels at a discounted price

SHORT NOVELLA

Man of the House

MEMOIR

HOPEFULLY EVER AFTER: Breast Cancer, Life and Me (true story about surviving breast cancer twice)

Printed in Great Britain
by Amazon

49117667R00116